PENGUIN ARCHIVE
The Daemon Lover

Shirley Jackson
1916–1965
A PENGUIN SINCE 1984

Shirley Jackson
The Daemon Lover

PENGUIN ARCHIVE

PENGUIN BOOKS

UK | USA | Canada | Ireland | Australia
India | New Zealand | South Africa

Penguin Books is part of the Penguin Random House group of companies whose addresses can be found at global.penguinrandomhouse.com.

Penguin Random House UK,
One Embassy Gardens, 8 Viaduct Gardens, London SW11 7BW

penguin.co.uk

Selected from *The Lottery and Other Stories*, *Just An Ordinary Day*, *Let Me Tell You* and *Dark Tales*, all published in Penguin Classics
This selection published in Penguin Classics 2025
003

Copyright © Laurence Jackson Hyman, J.S. Holly, Sarah Hyman DeWitt and Barry Hyman, 1967, 1977, 1996, 2015, 2016

No part of this book may be used or reproduced in any manner for the purpose of training artificial intelligence technologies or systems. In accordance with Article 4(3) of the DSM Directive 2019/790, Penguin Random House expressly reserves this work from the text and data mining exception.

Set in 11.2/13.75pt Dante MT Std
Typeset by Jouve (UK), Milton Keynes
Printed and bound in Great Britain by Clays Ltd, Elcograf S.p.A.

The authorized representative in the EEA is Penguin Random House Ireland, Morrison Chambers, 32 Nassau Street, Dublin D02 YH68

A CIP catalogue record for this book is available from the British Library

ISBN: 978–0–241–75213–5

Penguin Random House is committed to a sustainable future for our business, our readers and our planet. This book is made from Forest Stewardship Council® certified paper.

Contents

The Daemon Lover	1
Like Mother Used to Make	25
When Things Get Dark	39
Charles	47
Pillar of Salt	55
Murder on Miss Lederer's Birthday	77
Louisa, Please Come Home	87

The Daemon Lover

She had not slept well; from one-thirty, when Jamie left and she went lingeringly to bed, until seven, when she at last allowed herself to get up and make coffee, she had slept fitfully, stirring awake to open her eyes and look into the halfdarkness, remembering over and over, slipping again into a feverish dream. She spent almost an hour over her coffee – they were to have a real breakfast on the way – and then, unless she wanted to dress early, had nothing to do. She washed her coffee cup and made the bed, looking carefully over the clothes she planned to wear, worried unnecessarily, at the window, over whether it would be a fine day. She sat down to read, thought that she might write a letter to her sister instead, and began, in her finest handwriting, 'Dearest Anne, by the time you get this I will be married. Doesn't it sound funny? I can hardly believe it myself, but when I tell you how it happened, you'll see it's even stranger than that . . .'

Sitting, pen in hand, she hesitated over what to say next, read the lines already written, and tore up the letter. She went to the window and saw that it was undeniably a fine day. It occurred to her that perhaps she ought not to wear the blue silk dress; it was too plain, almost severe, and she wanted to be soft, feminine. Anxiously she pulled through the dresses in the closet, and hesitated over a print she had worn the summer before; it was too young for her, and it had a ruffled neck, and it was very early in the year for a print dress, but still . . .

She hung the two dresses side by side on the outside of the closet door and opened the glass doors carefully closed upon the small closet that was her kitchenette. She turned on the burner under the coffeepot, and went to the window; it was sunny. When the coffeepot began to crackle she came back and poured herself coffee, into a clean cup. I'll have a headache if I don't get some solid food soon, she thought, all this coffee, smoking too much, no real breakfast. A headache on her wedding day; she went and got the tin box of aspirin from the bathroom closet and slipped it into her blue pocketbook. She'd have to change to a brown pocketbook if she wore the print dress, and the only brown pocketbook she had was shabby. Helplessly, she stood looking from the blue pocketbook to the print dress, and then put the pocketbook down and went and got her coffee and sat down near the window, drinking her coffee, and looking carefully around the one-room apartment. They planned to come back here tonight and everything must be correct. With sudden horror she realized that she had forgotten to put clean sheets on the bed; the laundry was freshly back and she took clean sheets and pillow cases from the top shelf of the closet and stripped the bed,

The Daemon Lover

working quickly to avoid thinking consciously of why she was changing the sheets. The bed was a studio bed, with a cover to make it look like a couch, and when it was finished no one would have known she had just put clean sheets on it. She took the old sheets and pillow cases into the bathroom and stuffed them down into the hamper, and put the bathroom towels in the hamper too, and clean towels on the bathroom racks. Her coffee was cold when she came back to it, but she drank it anyway.

When she looked at the clock, finally, and saw that it was after nine, she began at last to hurry. She took a bath, and used one of the clean towels, which she put into the hamper and replaced with a clean one. She dressed carefully, all her underwear fresh and most of it new; she put everything she had worn the day before, including her nightgown, into the hamper. When she was ready for her dress, she hesitated before the closet door. The blue dress was certainly decent, and clean, and fairly becoming, but she had worn it several times with Jamie, and there was nothing about it which made it special for a wedding day. The print dress was overly pretty, and new to Jamie, and yet wearing such a print this early in the year was certainly rushing the season. Finally she thought, This is my wedding day, I can dress as I please, and she took the print dress down from the hanger. When she slipped it on over her head it felt fresh and light, but when she looked at herself in the mirror she remembered that the ruffles around the neck did not show her throat to any great advantage, and the wide swinging skirt looked irresistibly made for a girl, for someone who would run freely, dance, swing it with her hips when she walked. Looking at herself in the mirror she thought with revulsion, It's as though I was trying to make myself look prettier than I am, just for him; he'll think I want to look younger because he's marrying me; and she tore the print dress off so quickly that a seam under the arm ripped. In the old blue dress she felt comfortable and familiar, but unexciting. It isn't what you're wearing that matters, she told herself firmly, and turned in dismay to the closet to see if there might be anything else. There was nothing even remotely suitable for her marrying Jamie, and for a minute she thought of going out quickly to some little shop nearby, to get a dress. Then she saw that it was close on ten, and she had no time for more than her hair and her make-up. Her hair was easy, pulled back into a knot at the nape of her neck, but her make-up was another delicate balance between looking as well as possible, and deceiving as little. She could not try to disguise the sallowness of her skin, or the lines around her eyes, today, when it might look as though she were only doing it for her wedding, and yet she could not bear the thought of Jamie's bringing to marriage anyone who looked haggard and lined. You're thirty-four years old after *all,* she told herself cruelly in the bathroom mirror. Thirty, it said on the license.

It was two minutes after ten; she was not satisfied with her clothes, her face, her apartment. She heated the coffee again and sat down in the chair by the window.

Can't do anything more now, she thought, no sense trying to improve anything the last minute.

Reconciled, settled, she tried to think of Jamie and could not see his face clearly, or hear his voice. It's always that way with someone you love, she thought, and let her mind slip past today and tomorrow, into the farther future, when Jamie was established with his writing and she had given up her job, the golden house-in-the-country future they had been preparing for the last week. 'I used to be a wonderful cook,' she had promised Jamie, 'with a little time and practice I could remember how to make angel-food cake. And fried chicken,' she said, knowing how the words would stay in Jamie's mind, half-tenderly. 'And Hollandaise sauce.'

Ten-thirty. She stood up and went purposefully to the phone. She dialed, and waited, and the girl's metallic voice said, '. . . the time will be exactly ten-twenty-nine.' Half-consciously she set her clock back a minute; she was remembering her own voice saying last night, in the doorway: 'Ten o'clock then. I'll be ready. Is it really *true*?'

And Jamie laughing down the hallway.

By eleven o'clock she had sewed up the ripped seam in the print dress and put her sewing-box away carefully in the closet. With the print dress on, she was sitting by the window drinking another cup of coffee. I could have taken more time over my dressing after all, she thought; but by now it was so late he might come any minute, and she did not dare try to repair anything without starting all over. There was nothing to eat in the apartment except the food she had carefully stocked up for their life beginning together: the unopened package of bacon, the dozen eggs in their box, the unopened bread and the unopened butter; they were for breakfast tomorrow. She thought of running downstairs to the drugstore for something to eat, leaving a note on the door. Then she decided to wait a little longer.

By eleven-thirty she was so dizzy and weak that she had to go downstairs. If Jamie had had a phone she would have called him then. Instead, she opened her desk and wrote a note: 'Jamie, have gone downstairs to the drugstore. Back in five minutes.' Her pen leaked onto her fingers and she went into the bathroom and washed, using a clean towel which she replaced. She tacked the note on the door, surveyed the apartment once more to make sure that everything was perfect, and closed the door without locking it, in case he should come.

In the drugstore she found that there was nothing she wanted to eat except more coffee, and she left it half-finished because she suddenly realized that Jamie was probably upstairs waiting and impatient, anxious to get started.

But upstairs everything was prepared and quiet, as she had left it, her note unread on the door, the air in the apartment a little stale from too many cigarettes. She opened the window and sat down next to it until she realized that she had been asleep and it was twenty minutes to one.

The Daemon Lover

Now, suddenly, she was frightened. Waking without preparation into the room of waiting and readiness, everything clean and untouched since ten o'clock, she was frightened, and felt an urgent need to hurry. She got up from the chair and almost ran across the room to the bathroom, dashed cold water on her face, and used a clean towel; this time she put the towel carelessly back on the rack without changing it; time enough for that later. Hatless, still in the print dress with a coat thrown on over it, the wrong blue pocketbook with the aspirin inside in her hand, she locked the apartment door behind her, no note this time, and ran down the stairs. She caught a taxi on the corner and gave the driver Jamie's address.

It was no distance at all; she could have walked it if she had not been so weak, but in the taxi she suddenly realized how imprudent it would be to drive brazenly up to Jamie's door, demanding him. She asked the driver, therefore, to let her off at a corner near Jamie's address and, after paying him, waited till he drove away before she started to walk down the block. She had never been here before; the building was pleasant and old, and Jamie's name was not on any of the mailboxes in the vestibule, nor on the doorbells. She checked the address; it was right, and finally she rang the bell marked 'Superintendent.' After a minute or two the door buzzer rang and she opened the door and went into the dark hall where she hesitated until a door at the end opened and someone said, 'Yes?'

She knew at the same moment that she had no idea

what to ask, so she moved forward toward the figure waiting against the light of the open doorway. When she was very near, the figure said, 'Yes?' again and she saw that it was a man in his shirtsleeves, unable to see her any more clearly than she could see him.

With sudden courage she said, 'I'm trying to get in touch with someone who lives in this building and I can't find the name outside.'

'What's the name you wanted?' the man asked, and she realized that she would have to answer.

'James Harris,' she said. 'Harris.'

The man was silent for a minute and then he said, 'Harris.' He turned around to the room inside the lighted doorway and said, 'Margie, come here a minute.'

'What now?' a voice said from inside, and after a wait long enough for someone to get out of a comfortable chair a woman joined him in the doorway, regarding the dark hall. 'Lady here,' the man said. 'Lady looking for a guy name of Harris, lives here. Anyone in the building?'

'No,' the woman said. Her voice sounded amused. 'No men named Harris here.'

'Sorry,' the man said. He started to close the door. 'You got the wrong house, lady,' he said, and added in a lower voice, 'or the wrong guy,' and he and the woman laughed.

When the door was almost shut and she was alone in the dark hall she said to the thin lighted crack still showing, 'But he *does* live here; I know it.'

'Look,' the woman said, opening the door again a little, 'it happens all the time.'

'Please don't make any mistake,' she said, and her voice was very dignified, with thirty-four years of accumulated pride. 'I'm afraid you don't understand.'

'What did he look like?' the woman said wearily, the door still only part open.

'He's rather tall, and fair. He wears a blue suit very often. He's a writer.'

'No,' the woman said, and then, 'Could he have lived on the third floor?'

'I'm not sure.'

'There was a fellow,' the woman said reflectively. 'He wore a blue suit a lot, lived on the third floor for a while. The Roysters lent him their apartment while they were visiting her folks upstate.'

'That might be it; I thought, though . . .'

'This one wore a blue suit mostly, but I don't know how tall he was,' the woman said. 'He stayed there about a month.'

'A month ago is when –'

'You ask the Roysters,' the woman said. 'They come back this morning. Apartment 3B.'

The door closed, definitely. The hall was very dark and the stairs looked darker.

On the second floor there was a little light from a skylight far above. The apartment doors lined up, four on the floor, uncommunicative and silent. There was a bottle of milk outside 2C.

On the third floor, she waited for a minute. There

was the sound of music beyond the door of 3B, and she could hear voices. Finally she knocked, and knocked again. The door was opened and the music swept out at her, an early afternoon symphony broadcast. 'How do you do,' she said politely to this woman in the doorway. 'Mrs Royster?'

'That's right.' The woman was wearing a housecoat and last night's make-up.

'I wonder if I might talk to you for a minute?'

'Sure,' Mrs Royster said, not moving.

'About Mr Harris.'

'*What* Mr Harris?' Mrs Royster said flatly.

'Mr James Harris. The gentleman who borrowed your apartment.'

'O Lord,' Mrs Royster said. She seemed to open her eyes for the first time. 'What'd he do?'

'Nothing. I'm just trying to get in touch with him.'

'O Lord,' Mrs Royster said again. Then she opened the door wider and said, 'Come in,' and then, 'Ralph!'

Inside, the apartment was still full of music, and there were suitcases half-unpacked on the couch, on the chairs, on the floor. A table in the corner was spread with the remains of a meal, and the young man sitting there, for a minute resembling Jamie, got up and came across the room.

'What about it?' he said.

'Mr Royster,' she said. It was difficult to talk against the music. 'The superintendent downstairs told me that this was where Mr James Harris has been living.'

'Sure,' he said. 'If that was his name.'

The Daemon Lover

'I thought you lent him the apartment,' she said, surprised.

'*I* don't know anything about him,' Mr Royster said. 'He's one of Dottie's friends.'

'Not *my* friends,' Mrs Royster said. 'No friend of mine.' She had gone over to the table and was spreading peanut butter on a piece of bread. She took a bite and said thickly, waving the bread and peanut butter at her husband. 'Not *my* friend.'

'You picked him up at one of those damn meetings,' Mr Royster said. He shoved a suitcase off the chair next to the radio and sat down, picking up a magazine from the floor next to him. 'I never said more'n ten words to him.'

'You said it was okay to lend him the place,' Mrs Royster said before she took another bite. 'You never said a word against him, after *all*.'

'*I* don't say anything about *your* friends,' Mr Royster said.

'If he'd of been a friend of mine you would have said *plenty*, believe me,' Mrs Royster said darkly. She took another bite and said, 'Believe me, he would have said *plenty*.'

'That's all I want to hear,' Mr Royster said, over the top of the magazine. 'No more, now.'

'You see.' Mrs Royster pointed the bread and peanut butter at her husband. 'That's the way it is, day and night.'

There was silence except for the music bellowing out of the radio next to Mr Royster, and then she said, in a voice she hardly trusted to be heard over the radio noise, 'Has he gone, then?'

'Who?' Mrs Royster demanded, looking up from the peanut butter jar.

'Mr James Harris.'

'Him? He must've left this morning, before we got back. No sign of him anywhere.'

'Gone?'

'Everything was fine, though, perfectly fine. I told you,' she said to Mr Royster, 'I told you he'd take care of everything fine. I can always tell.'

'You were lucky,' Mr Royster said.

'Not a thing out of place,' Mrs Royster said. She waved her bread and peanut butter inclusively. 'Everything just the way we left it,' she said.

'Do you know where he is now?'

'Not the slightest idea,' Mrs Royster said cheerfully. 'But, like I said, he left everything fine. Why?' she asked suddenly. 'You looking for *him*?'

'It's very important.'

'I'm sorry he's not here,' Mrs Royster said. She stepped forward politely when she saw her visitor turn toward the door.

'Maybe the super saw him,' Mr Royster said into the magazine.

When the door was closed behind her the hall was dark again, but the sound of the radio was deadened. She was halfway down the first flight of stairs when the door was opened and Mrs Royster shouted down the stairwell, 'If I see him I'll tell him you were looking for him.'

What can I do? she thought, out on the street again. It was impossible to go home, not with Jamie somewhere

The Daemon Lover

between here and there. She stood on the sidewalk so long that a woman, leaning out of a window across the way, turned and called to someone inside to come and see. Finally, on an impulse, she went into the small delicatessen next door to the apartment house, on the side that led to her own apartment. There was a small man reading a newspaper, leaning against the counter; when she came in he looked up and came down inside the counter to meet her.

Over the glass case of cold meats and cheese she said, timidly, 'I'm trying to get in touch with a man who lived in the apartment house next door, and I just wondered if you know him.'

'Whyn't you ask the people there?' the man said, his eyes narrow, inspecting her.

It's because I'm not buying anything, she thought, and she said, 'I'm sorry. I asked them, but they don't know anything about him. They think he left this morning.'

'I don't know what you want *me* to do,' he said, moving a little back toward his newspaper. 'I'm not here to keep track of guys going in and out next door.'

She said quickly, 'I thought you might have noticed, that's all. He would have been coming past here, a little before ten o'clock. He was rather tall, and he usually wore a blue suit.'

'Now how many men in blue suits go past here every day, lady?' the man demanded. 'You think I got nothing to do but –'

'I'm sorry,' she said. She heard him say, 'For God's sake,' as she went out the door.

As she walked toward the corner, she thought, he must have come this way, it's the way he'd go to get to my house, it's the only way for him to walk. She tried to think of Jamie: where would he have crossed the street? What sort of person was he actually – would he cross in front of his own apartment: house, at random in the middle of the block, at the corner?

On the corner was a newsstand; they might have seen him there. She hurried on and waited while a man bought a paper and a woman asked directions. When the newsstand man looked at her she said, 'Can you possibly tell me if a rather tall young man in a blue suit went past here this morning around ten o'clock?' When the man only looked at her, his eyes wide and his mouth a little open, she thought, he thinks it's a joke, or a trick, and she said urgently, 'It's very important, please believe me. I'm not teasing you.'

'*Look*, lady,' the man began, and she said eagerly, 'He's a writer. He might have bought magazines here.'

'What you want him for?' the man asked. He looked at her, smiling, and she realized that there was another man waiting in back of her and the newsdealer's smile included him. 'Never mind,' she said, but the newsdealer said, 'Listen maybe he did come by here.' His smile was knowing and his eyes shifted over her shoulder to the man in back of her. She was suddenly horribly aware of her over-young print dress, and pulled her coat around her quickly. The newsdealer said, with vast thoughtfulness, 'Now I don't know for sure, mind you, but there might have

The Daemon Lover

been someone like your gentleman friend coming by this morning.'

'About ten?'

'About ten,' the newsdealer agreed. 'Tall fellow, blue suit. I wouldn't be at all surprised.'

'Which way did he go?' she said eagerly. 'Uptown?'

'Uptown,' the newsdealer said, nodding. 'He went uptown. That's just exactly it. What can I do for you, sir?'

She stepped back, holding her coat around her. The man who had been standing behind her looked at her over his shoulder and then he and the newsdealer looked at one another. She wondered for a minute whether or not to tip the newsdealer but when both men began to laugh she moved hurriedly on across the street.

Uptown, she thought, that's right, and she started up the avenue, thinking: He wouldn't have to cross the avenue, just go up six blocks and turn down my street, so long as he started uptown. About a block farther on she passed a florist's shop; there was a wedding display in the window and she thought, This is my wedding day after all, he might have gotten flowers to bring me, and she went inside. The florist came out of the back of the shop, smiling and sleek, and she said, before he could speak, so that he wouldn't have a chance to think she was buying anything: 'It's *terribly* important that I get in touch with a gentleman who may have stopped in here to buy flowers this morning. *Terribly* important.'

She stopped for breath, and the florist said, 'Yes, what sort of flowers were they?'

'I don't know,' she said, surprised. 'He never –' She stopped and said, 'He was a rather tall young man, in a blue suit. It was about ten o'clock.'

'I see,' the florist said. 'Well, *really*, I'm afraid . . .'

'But it's *so* important,' she said. 'He may have been in a hurry,' she added helpfully.

'Well,' the florist said. He smiled genially, showing all his small teeth. 'For a *lady*,' he said. He went to a stand and opened a large book. 'Where were they to be sent?' he asked.

'Why,' she said, 'I don't think he'd have sent them. You see, he was coming – that is, he'd *bring* them.'

'Madam,' the florist said; he was offended. His smile became deprecatory, and he went on, 'Really, you must realize that unless I have *something* to go on . . .'

'*Please* try to remember,' she begged. 'He was tall, and had a blue suit, and it was about ten this morning.'

The florist closed his eyes, one finger to his mouth, and thought deeply. Then he shook his head. 'I simply *can't*,' he said.

'Thank you,' she said despondently, and started for the door, when the florist said, in a shrill, excited voice, 'Wait! Wait just a moment, madam.' She turned and the florist, thinking again, said finally, 'Chrysanthemums?' He looked at her inquiringly.

'Oh, *no*,' she said; her voice shook a little and she waited for a minute before she went on. 'Not for an occasion like this, I'm sure.'

The Daemon Lover

The florist tightened his lips and looked away coldly. 'Well, of *course* I don't know the *occasion*,' he said, 'but I'm almost certain that the gentleman you were inquiring for came in this morning and purchased one dozen chrysanthemums. No delivery.'

'You're *sure?*' she asked.

'Positive,' the florist said emphatically. 'That was absolutely the man.' He smiled brilliantly, and she smiled back and said, 'Well, thank you very much.'

He escorted her to the door. 'Nice corsage?' he said, as they went through the shop. 'Red roses? Gardenias?'

'It was very kind of you to help me,' she said at the door.

'Ladies always look their best in flowers,' he said, bending his head toward her. 'Orchids, perhaps?'

'No, thank you,' she said, and he said, 'I hope you find your young man,' and gave it a nasty sound.

Going on up the street she thought, Everyone thinks it's so *funny:* and she pulled her coat tighter around her, so that only the ruffle around the bottom of the print dress was showing.

There was a policeman on the corner, and she thought, Why don't I go to the police – you go to the police for a missing person. And then thought, What a fool I'd look like. She had a quick picture of herself standing in a police station, saying, 'Yes, we were going to be married today, but he didn't come,' and the policemen, three or four of them standing around listening, looking at her, at the print dress, at her too-bright make-up, smiling at one another. She couldn't tell them any more than that, could not say, 'Yes, it looks silly, doesn't it, me all dressed up and trying to find the young man who promised to marry me, but what about all of it you don't know? I have more than this, more than you can see: talent, perhaps, and humor of a sort, and I'm a lady and I have pride and affection and delicacy and a certain clear view of life that might make a man satisfied and productive and happy; there's more than you think when you look at me.'

The police were obviously impossible, leaving out Jamie and what he might think when he heard she'd set the police after him. 'No, no,' she said aloud, hurrying her steps, and someone passing stopped and looked after her.

On the coming corner – she was three blocks from her own street – was a shoeshine stand, an old man sitting almost asleep in one of the chairs. She stopped in front of him and waited, and after a minute he opened his eyes and smiled at her.

'Look,' she said, the words coming before she thought of them, 'I'm sorry to bother you, but I'm looking for a young man who came up this way about ten this morning, did you see him?' And she began her description, 'Tall, blue suit, carrying a bunch of flowers?'

The old man began to nod before she was finished. 'I saw him,' he said. 'Friend of yours?'

'Yes,' she said, and smiled back involuntarily.

The old man blinked his eyes and said, 'I remember I thought, You're going to see your girl, young fellow.

The Daemon Lover

They all go to see their girls,' he said, and shook his head tolerantly.

'Which way did he go? Straight on up the avenue?'

'That's right,' the old man said. 'Got a shine, had his flowers, all dressed up, in an awful hurry. You got a girl, I thought.'

'Thank you,' she said, fumbling in her pocket for her loose change.

'She sure must of been glad to see him, the way he looked,' the old man said.

'Thank you,' she said again, and brought her hand empty from her pocket.

For the first time she was really sure he would be waiting for her, and she hurried up the three blocks, the skirt of the print dress swinging under her coat, and turned into her own block. From the corner she could not see her own windows, could not see Jamie looking out, waiting for her, and going down the block she was almost running to get to him. Her key trembled in her fingers at the downstairs door, and as she glanced into the drugstore she thought of her panic, drinking coffee there this morning, and almost laughed. At her own door she could wait no longer, but began to say, 'Jamie, I'm here, I was so worried,' even before the door was open.

Her own apartment was waiting for her, silent, barren, afternoon shadows lengthening from the window. For a minute she saw only the empty coffee cup, thought, He has been here waiting, before she recognized it as her own, left from the morning.

She looked all over the room, into the closet, into the bathroom.

'I never saw him,' the clerk in the drugstore said. 'I know because I would of noticed the flowers. No one like that's been in.'

The old man at the shoeshine stand woke up again to see her standing in front of him. 'Hello again,' he said, and smiled.

'Are you *sure?*' she demanded. 'Did he go on up the avenue?'

'I watched him,' the old man said, dignified against her tone. 'I thought, There's a young man's got a girl, and I watched him right into the house.'

'What house?' she said remotely.

'Right there,' the old man said. He leaned forward to point. 'The next block. With his flowers and his shine and going to see his girl. Right into her house.'

'Which one?' she said.

'About the middle of the block,' the old man said. He looked at her with suspicion, and said, 'What you trying to do, anyway?'

She almost ran, without stopping to say 'Thank you.' Up on the next block she walked quickly, searching the houses from the outside to see if Jamie looked from a window, listening to hear his laughter somewhere inside.

A woman was sitting in front of one of the houses, pushing a baby carriage monotonously back and forth the length of her arm. The baby inside slept, moving back and forth.

The Daemon Lover

The question was fluent, by now. 'I'm sorry, but did you see a young man go into one of these houses about ten this morning? He was tall, wearing a blue suit, carrying a bunch of flowers.'

A boy about twelve stopped to listen, turning intently from one to the other, occasionally glancing at the baby.

'Listen,' the woman said tiredly, 'the kid has his bath at ten. Would I see strange men walking around? I ask you.'

'Big bunch of flowers?' the boy asked, pulling at her coat. 'Big bunch of flowers? I seen him, missus.'

She looked down and the boy grinned insolently at her. 'Which house did he go in?' she asked wearily.

'You gonna divorce him?' the boy asked insistently.

'That's not nice to ask the lady,' the woman rocking the carriage said.

'Listen,' the boy said, 'I seen him. He went in there.' He pointed to the house next door. 'I followed him,' the boy said. 'He give me a quarter.' The boy dropped his voice to a growl, and said, ' "This is a big day for me, kid," he says. Give me a quarter.'

She gave him a dollar bill. 'Where?' she said.

'Top floor,' the boy said. 'I followed him till he give me the quarter. Way to the top.' He backed up the sidewalk, out of reach, with the dollar bill. 'You gonna divorce him?' he asked again.

'Was he carrying flowers?'

'Yeah,' the boy said. He began to screech. 'You gonna divorce him, missus? You got something on him?' He went careening down the street, howling, 'She's got something on the poor guy,' and the woman rocking the baby laughed.

The street door of the apartment house was unlocked; there were no bells in the outer vestibule, and no lists of names. The stairs were narrow and dirty; there were two doors on the top floor. The front one was the right one; there was a crumpled florist's paper on the floor outside the door, and a knotted paper ribbon, like a clue, like the final clue in the paper-chase.

She knocked, and thought she heard voices inside, and she thought, suddenly, with terror, What shall I say if Jamie is there, if he comes to the door? The voices seemed suddenly still. She knocked again and there was silence, except for something that might have been laughter far away. He could have seen me from the window, she thought, it's the front apartment and that little boy made a dreadful noise. She waited, and knocked again, but there was silence.

Finally she went to the other door on the floor, and knocked. The door swung open beneath her hand and she saw the empty attic room, bare lath on the walls, floorboards unpainted. She stepped just inside, looking around; the room was filled with bags of plaster, piles of old newspapers, a broken trunk. There was a noise which she suddenly realized as a rat, and then she saw it, sitting very close to her, near the wall, its evil face alert, bright eyes watching her. She stumbled in her haste to be out with the door closed, and the skirt of the print dress caught and tore.

The Daemon Lover

She knew there was someone inside the other apartment, because she was sure she could hear low voices and sometimes laughter. She came back many times, every day for the first week. She came on her way to work, in the mornings; in the evenings, on her way to dinner alone, but no matter how often or how firmly she knocked, no one ever came to the door.

Like Mother Used to Make

David Turner, who did everything in small quick movements, hurried from the bus stop down the avenue toward his street. He reached the grocery on the corner and hesitated; there had been something. Butter, he remembered with relief; this morning, all the way up the avenue to his bus stop, he had been telling himself butter, don't forget butter coming home tonight, when you pass the grocery remember butter. He went into the grocery and waited his turn, examining the cans on the shelves. Canned pork sausage was back, and corned-beef hash. A tray full of rolls caught his eye, and then the woman ahead of him went out and the clerk turned to him.

'How much is butter?' David asked cautiously.

'Eighty-nine,' the clerk said easily.

'Eighty-nine?' David frowned.

'That's what it is,' the clerk said. He looked past David at the next customer.

'Quarter of a pound, please,' David said. 'And a half-dozen rolls.'

Carrying his package home he thought, I really ought not to trade there any more; you'd think they'd know me well enough to be more courteous.

There was a letter from his mother in the mailbox. He stuck it into the top of the bag of rolls and went upstairs to the third floor. No light in Marcia's apartment, the only other apartment on the floor. David turned to his own door and unlocked it, snapping on the light as he came in the door. Tonight, as every night when he came home, the apartment looked warm and friendly and good; the little foyer, with the neat small table and four careful chairs, and the bowl of little marigolds against the pale green walls David had painted himself; beyond, the kitchenette, and beyond that, the big room where David read and slept and the ceiling of which was a perpetual trouble to him; the plaster was falling in one corner and no power on earth could make it less noticeable. David consoled himself for the plaster constantly with the thought that perhaps if he had not taken an apartment in an old brownstone the plaster would not be falling, but then, too, for the money he paid he could not have a foyer and a big room and a kitchenette, anywhere else.

He put his bag down on the table and put the butter away in the refrigerator and the rolls in the breadbox. He folded the empty bag and put it in a drawer in the kitchenette. Then he hung his coat in the hall closet and went into the big room, which he called his living-room, and lighted the desk light. His word for the room, in his own mind, was 'charming.' He had always been partial to yellows and browns, and he had painted the desk and the bookcases and the end tables himself, had even painted the walls, and had hunted around the city for the exact tweedish tan drapes he had in mind. The

Like Mother Used to Make

room satisfied him: the rug was a rich dark brown that picked up the darkest thread in the drapes, the furniture was almost yellow, the cover on the studio couch and the lampshades were orange. The rows of plants on the window sills gave the touch of green the room needed; right now David was looking for an ornament to set on the end table, but he had his heart set on a low translucent green bowl for more marigolds, and such things cost more than he could afford, after the silverware.

He could not come into this room without feeling that it was the most comfortable home he had ever had; tonight, as always, he let his eyes move slowly around the room, from couch to drapes to bookcase, imagined the green bowl on the end table, and sighed as he turned to the desk. He took his pen from the holder, and a sheet of the neat notepaper sitting in one of the desk cubbyholes, and wrote carefully: 'Dear Marcia, don't forget you're coming for dinner tonight. I'll expect you about six.' He signed the note with a 'D' and picked up the key to Marcia's apartment which lay in the flat pencil tray on his desk. He had a key to Marcia's apartment because she was never home when her laundryman came, or when the man came to fix the refrigerator or the telephone or the windows, and someone had to let them in because the landlord was reluctant to climb three flights of stairs with the pass key. Marcia had never suggested having a key to David's apartment, and he had never offered her one; it pleased him to have only one key to his home, and that safely in his own pocket; it had a pleasant feeling to him, solid and small, the only way into his warm fine home.

He left his front door open and went down the dark hall to the other apartment. He opened the door with his key and turned on the light. This apartment was not agreeable for him to come into; it was exactly the same as his: foyer, kitchenette, living-room, and it reminded him constantly of his first day in his own apartment, when the thought of the careful home-making to be done had left him very close to despair. Marcia's home was bare and at random; an upright piano a friend had given her recently stood crookedly, half in the foyer, because the little room was too narrow and the big room was too cluttered for it to sit comfortably anywhere; Marcia's bed was unmade and a pile of dirty laundry lay on the floor. The window had been open all day and papers had blown wildly around the floor. David closed the window, hesitated over the papers, and then moved away quickly. He put the note on the piano keys and locked the door behind him.

In his own apartment he settled down happily to making dinner. He had made a little pot roast for dinner the night before; most of it was still in the refrigerator and he sliced it in fine thin slices and arranged it on a plate with parsley. His plates were orange, almost the same color as the couch cover, and it was pleasant to him to arrange a salad, with the lettuce on the orange plate, and the thin slices of cucumber. He put coffee on to cook, and sliced potatoes to fry, and then, with his dinner cooking agreeably and the window open to lose the odor of the frying potatoes, he set lovingly to arranging his table. First, the tablecloth, pale green, of course. And the two fresh green napkins. The orange plates and the precise cup and saucer at each place. The plate of rolls in the center, and the odd salt and pepper shakers, like two green frogs. Two glasses – they came from the five-and-ten, but they had thin green bands around them – and finally, with great care, the silverware. Gradually, tenderly, David was buying himself a complete set of silverware; starting out modestly with a service for two, he had added to it until now he had well over a service for four, although not quite a service for six, lacking salad forks and soup spoons. He had chosen a sedate, pretty pattern, one that would be fine with any sort of table setting, and each morning he gloried in a breakfast that started with a shining silver spoon for his grapefruit, and had a compact butter knife for his toast and a solid heavy knife to break his eggshell, and a fresh silver spoon for his coffee, which he sugared with a particular spoon meant only for sugar. The silverware lay in a tarnish-proof box on a high shelf all to itself, and David lifted it down carefully to take out a service for two. It made a lavish display set out on the table – knives, forks, salad forks, more forks for the pie, a spoon to each place, and the special serving pieces – the sugar spoon, the large serving spoons for the potatoes and the salad, the fork for the meat, and the pie fork. When the table held as much silverware as two people could possibly use he put the box back on the shelf and stood back, checking everything and admiring the table, shining and clean.

Then he went into his living-room to read his mother's letter and wait for Marcia.

The potatoes were done before Marcia came, and then suddenly the door burst open and Marcia arrived with a shout and fresh air and disorder. She was a tall handsome girl with a loud voice, wearing a dirty raincoat, and she said, 'I didn't forget, Davie, I'm just late as usual. What's for dinner? You're not mad, are you?'

David got up and came over to take her coat. 'I left a note for you,' he said.

'Didn't see it,' Marcia said. 'Haven't been home. Something smells good.'

'Fried potatoes,' David said. 'Everything's ready.'

'Golly.' Marcia fell into a chair to sit with her legs stretched out in front of her and her arms hanging. 'I'm tired,' she said. 'It's cold out.'

'It was getting colder when I came home,' David said. He was putting dinner on the table, the platter of meat, the salad, the bowl of fried potatoes. He walked quietly back and forth from the kitchenette to the table, avoiding Marcia's feet. 'I don't believe you've been here since I got my silverware,' he said.

Marcia swung around to the table and picked up a spoon. 'It's beautiful,' she said, running her finger along the pattern. 'Pleasure to eat with it.'

'Dinner's ready,' David said. He pulled her chair out for her and waited for her to sit down.

Marcia was always hungry; she put meat and potatoes and salad on her plate without admiring the serving silver, and started to eat enthusiastically.

Like Mother Used to Make

'Everything's beautiful,' she said once. 'Food is wonderful, Davie.'

'I'm glad you like it,' David said. He liked the feel of the fork in his hand, even the sight of the fork moving up to Marcia's mouth.

Marcia waved her hand largely. 'I mean everything,' she said, 'furniture, and nice place you have here, and dinner, and everything.'

'I *like* things this way,' David said.

'I know you do.' Marcia's voice was mournful. 'Someone should teach me, I guess.'

'You *ought* to keep your home neater,' David said. 'You ought to get curtains at least, and keep your windows shut.'

'I never remember,' she said. 'Davie, you are the most *wonderful* cook.' She pushed her plate away, and sighed.

David blushed happily. 'I'm glad you like it,' he said again, and then he laughed. 'I made a pie last night.'

'A pie.' Marcia looked at him for a minute and then she said, 'Apple?'

David shook his head, and she said, 'Pineapple?' and he shook his head again, and, because he could not wait to tell her, said, 'Cherry.'

'My *god!*' Marcia got up and followed him into the kitchen and looked over his shoulder while he took the pie carefully out of the breadbox. 'Is this the first pie you ever made?'

'I've made two before,' David admitted, 'but this one turned out better than the others.'

She watched happily while he cut large pieces of pie

and put them on other orange plates, and then she carried her own plate back to the table, tasted the pie, and made wordless gestures of appreciation. David tasted his pie and said critically, 'I think it's a little sour. I ran out of sugar.'

'It's perfect,' Marcia said. 'I always loved a cherry pie really *sour*. This isn't sour enough, even.'

David cleared the table and poured the coffee, and as he was setting the coffeepot back on the stove Marcia said, 'My doorbell's ringing.' She opened the apartment door and listened, and they could both hear the ringing in her apartment. She pressed the buzzer in David's apartment that opened the downstairs door, and far away they could hear heavy footsteps starting up the stairs. Marcia left the apartment door open and came back to her coffee. 'Landlord, most likely,' she said. 'I didn't pay my rent again.' When the footsteps reached the top of the last staircase Marcia yelled, 'Hello?' leaning back in her chair to see out the door into the hall. Then she said, 'Why, Mr Harris.' She got up and went to the door and held out her hand. 'Come in,' she said.

'I just thought I'd stop by,' Mr Harris said. He was a very large man and his eyes rested curiously on the coffee cups and empty plates on the table. 'I don't want to interrupt your dinner.'

'*That's* all right,' Marcia said, pulling him into the room. 'It's just Davie. Davie, this is Mr Harris, he works in my office. This is Mr Turner.'

'How do you do,' David said politely, and the man looked at him carefully and said, 'How do you do?'

Like Mother Used to Make

'Sit down, sit down,' Marcia was saying, pushing a chair forward. 'Davie, how about another cup for Mr Harris?'

'Please don't bother,' Mr Harris said quickly, 'I just thought I'd stop by.'

While David was taking out another cup and saucer and getting a spoon down from the tarnish-proof silverbox, Marcia said, 'You like homemade pie?'

'Say,' Mr Harris said admiringly, 'I've forgotten what homemade pie *looks* like.'

'Davie,' Marcia called cheerfully, 'how about cutting Mr Harris a piece of that pie?'

Without answering, David took a fork out of the silverbox and got down an orange plate and put a piece of pie on it. His plans for the evening had been vague; they had involved perhaps a movie if it were not too cold out, and at least a short talk with Marcia about the state of her home; Mr Harris was settling down in his chair and when David put the pie down silently in front of him he stared at it admiringly for a minute before he tasted it.

'Say,' he said finally, 'this is certainly some pie.' He looked at Marcia. 'This is really *good* pie,' he said.

'You like it?' Marcia asked modestly. She looked up at David and smiled at him over Mr Harris' head. 'I haven't made but two, three pies before,' she said.

David raised a hand to protest, but Mr Harris turned to him and demanded, 'Did you ever eat any better pie in your life?'

'I don't think Davie liked it much,' Marcia said wickedly, 'I think it was too sour for him.'

'I *like* a sour pie,' Mr Harris said. He looked suspiciously at David. 'A cherry pie's *got* to be sour.'

'I'm glad you like it, anyway,' Marcia said. Mr Harris ate the last mouthful of pie, finished his coffee, and sat back. 'I'm sure glad I dropped in,' he said to Marcia.

David's desire to be rid of Mr Harris had slid imperceptibly into an urgency to be rid of them both; his clean house, his nice silver, were not meant as vehicles for the kind of fatuous banter Marcia and Mr Harris were playing at together; almost roughly he took the coffee cup away from the arm Marcia had stretched across the table, took it out to the kitchenette and came back and put his hand on Mr Harris' cup.

'Don't bother, Davie, honestly,' Marcia said. She looked up, smiling again, as though she and David were conspirators against Mr Harris. 'I'll do them all tomorrow, honey,' she said.

'Sure,' Mr Harris said. He stood up. 'Let them wait. Let's go in and sit down where we can be comfortable.'

Marcia got up and led him into the living-room and they sat down on the studio couch. 'Come on in, Davie,' Marcia called.

The sight of his pretty table covered with dirty dishes and cigarette ashes held David. He carried the plates and cups and silverware into the kitchenette and stacked them in the sink and then, because he could not endure the thought of their sitting there any longer, with the dirt gradually hardening on them, he tied an apron on and began to wash them carefully. Now and then, while he was washing them and drying them and putting them

Like Mother Used to Make

away, Marcia would call to him, sometimes, 'Davie, what *are* you doing?' or, 'Davie, won't you stop all that and come sit down?' Once she said, 'Davie, I don't want you to wash all those dishes,' and Mr Harris said, 'Let him work, he's happy.'

David put the clean yellow cups and saucers back on the shelves – by now, Mr Harris' cup was unrecognizable; you could not tell, from the clean rows of cups, which one he had used or which one had been stained with Marcia's lipstick or which one had held David's coffee which he had finished in the kitchenette – and finally, taking the tarnish-proof box down, he put the silverware away. First the forks all went in together into the little grooves which held two forks each – later, when the set was complete, each groove would hold four forks – and then the spoons, stacked up neatly one on top of another in their own grooves, and the knives in even order, all facing the same way, in the special tapes in the lid of the box. Butter knives and serving spoons and the pie knife all went into their own places, and then David put the lid down on the lovely shining set and put the box back on the shelf. After wringing out the dishcloth and hanging up the dish towel and taking off his apron he was through, and he went slowly into the living-room. Marcia and Mr Harris were sitting close together on the studio couch, talking earnestly.

'My *father's* name was James,' Marcia was saying as David came in, as though she were clinching an argument. She turned around when David came in and said, 'Davie, you were so nice to do all those dishes yourself.'

'That's all right,' David said awkwardly. Mr Harris was looking at him impatiently.

'I should have helped you,' Marcia said. There was a silence, and then Marcia said, 'Sit down, Davie, won't you?'

David recognized her tone; it was the one hostesses used when they didn't know what else to say to you, or when you had come too early or stayed too late. It was the tone he had expected to use on Mr Harris.

'James and I were just talking about . . .' Marcia began and then stopped and laughed. 'What *were* we talking about?' she asked, turning to Mr Harris.

'Nothing much,' Mr Harris said. He was still watching David.

'Well,' Marcia said, letting her voice trail off. She turned to David and smiled brightly and then said, 'Well,' again.

Mr Harris picked up the ashtray from the end table and set it on the couch between himself and Marcia. He took a cigar out of his pocket and said to Marcia, 'Do you mind cigars?' and when Marcia shook her head he unwrapped the cigar tenderly and bit off the end. 'Cigar smoke's good for plants,' he said thickly, around the cigar, as he lighted it, and Marcia laughed.

David stood up. For a minute he thought he was going to say something that might start, 'Mr Harris, I'll thank you to . . .' but what he actually said, finally, with both Marcia and Mr Harris looking at him, was, 'Guess I better be getting along, Marcia.'

Mr Harris stood up and said heartily, 'Certainly have

Like Mother Used to Make

enjoyed meeting you.' He held out his hand and David shook hands limply.

'Guess I better be getting along,' he said again to Marcia, and she stood up and said, 'I'm sorry you have to leave so soon.'

'Lots of work to do,' David said, much more genially than he intended, and Marcia smiled at him again as though they were conspirators and went over to the desk and said, 'Don't forget your key.'

Surprised, David took the key of her apartment from her, said good night to Mr Harris, and went to the outside door.

'Good night, Davie honey,' Marcia called out, and David said 'Thanks for a simply *wonderful* dinner, Marcia,' and closed the door behind him.

He went down the hall and let himself into Marcia's apartment; the piano was still awry, the papers were still on the floor, the laundry scattered, the bed unmade. David sat down on the bed and looked around. It was cold, it was dirty, and as he thought miserably of his own warm home he heard faintly down the hall the sound of laughter and the scrape of a chair being moved. Then, still faintly, the sound of his radio. Wearily, David leaned over and picked up a paper from the floor, and then he began to gather them up one by one.

When Things Get Dark

Mrs Garden was sitting in the overstuffed chair in her furnished room, smoking. She was a young woman, not more than twenty-three or four. She was small and thin and she was wearing a light blue corduroy housecoat and had her hair in curlers. It was eleven in the morning. She was finishing her third cup of coffee from the pot on the electric plate. Beside her on the small table was a letter. When she put her cup down, she took up the single sheet of ruled letter paper and read it again. 'Dear Mrs Garden,' it said, 'I can't help feeling that right now you are in need of a friend. You seemed to be so strong and courageous when I met you, in spite of your great trouble, that I am sure your young heart will be equal to any burden. When things get dark, remember there are always friends thinking of you and wishing you well.' The letter was signed 'A. H.' After a minute Mrs Garden put it down on the table and went over to the dresser. She took her pocketbook out of it and, rummaging through it, found a match folder. On the inside of the folder was written 'Mrs Amelia Hope, III Mortimer Street, Brooklyn Hgts.'

Mrs Garden stood in front of the dresser for a minute, looking at herself in the glass. I won't show at all for a while, she thought. No one would know unless I told them. She turned, holding her arms high, to look at herself in profile. After a minute she walked across the room and got the letter and put it and the match folder in her pocketbook. She went to the closet and took down a dark blue suit and a white blouse, thinking, My clothes still fit me – all the nice things I bought and won't be able to wear. She dressed carefully pinning the tiny infantry insignia to her lapel, and took a dark blue hat out of the closet. When she was dressed she glanced around the room before she locked the door. She looked quiet and decent and worried. Out in the hall, she put the key in her pocketbook and went down the stairs.

All the way in the subway, Mrs Garden held the pocketbook quietly in her lap, looking out the windows into the darkness. When she reached the station where the subway guard had told her to get off, she got up and went out into the street, where she went to a newsstand and asked the way to the address. Then, still holding her pocketbook close to her, she walked to 111 Mortimer Street. It was an old house, clearly a rooming house, and it looked ugly and decayed. Mrs Garden went up the steps and rang the bell. When the landlady opened the door, Mrs Garden said, 'I want to see Mrs Amelia Hope, please.'

The landlady stood back and said, 'Second floor, in the back.'

Mrs Garden went up the wide staircase, the sort of staircase you would find in an old, beautiful house, to a second floor with a high-ceilinged hall and white plaster ornamental molding. There was one door toward the back, at the end of the long hall, and Mrs Garden knocked on it.

'Come in, please,' an old lady's voice said. Mrs Garden opened the door and stood just inside. For a minute it was hard for her to see, because she was facing a high, narrow window with long brown drapes down each side of it. Then she saw a small, old-fashioned desk with carved spindle legs in front of the window, and Mrs Hope sitting at it.

'I'm Mrs Garden. Do you remember me?'

Mrs Hope rose and came a step or two forward. 'Mrs Garden?' she said.

Mrs Garden opened her pocketbook and took out the letter. She held it out to Mrs Hope and said, 'I wanted to ask you about this.'

Mrs Hope looked at the letter and then at Mrs Garden. 'Won't you sit down?' she said. She gestured at a little gilt chair near the desk. 'You find me in a good deal of confusion,' she said. 'It seems that they clean my room later each day. You know,' she said, leaning forward to touch Mrs Garden on the knee, 'I pay a small sum extra each week to have my room cleaned *well* – really well, you know – and I think I'm going to have to speak to them about it. They don't do it at all as they should.'

Mrs Garden looked around. The narrow bed in one corner looked, at first, hardly disturbed, and then she saw that it had not been made up yet that morning. A cup with a tea bag in the saucer sat on the desk, and beside it a pad of ruled writing paper, like the paper Mrs Garden's letter was written on.

'I hope I didn't interrupt you at anything,' Mrs Garden said.

'Indeed not,' Mrs Hope said. She stood up and Mrs Garden realized that she was incredibly small. She was wearing a plain black dress with a red belt, and around her neck was a long rope of aromatic cedar beads. 'Will you have some candy?' she asked. She went over to the table by her bed and brought back a small glass dish of candy corn, which she set on the desk where Mrs Garden could reach it. 'I was just writing my letters,' she said.

'It's funny,' Mrs Garden said. 'I never expected to meet you again.'

'I'm sure I know you,' Mrs Hope said, 'but I can't quite remember where we met.' She was leaning forward, pleased and attentive.

Mrs Garden looked up, surprised. 'Why, on the bus. You were so nice to me.'

Mrs Hope glanced down at the letter on the desk. 'Certainly I remember now,' she said. 'You're the young lady with the child.'

'No,' Mrs Garden said. 'My husband had just left to be sent overseas. Mrs Hope, I need advice very badly.'

'It wasn't a child, come to think of it,' Mrs Hope said. 'It was a sick mother. We women are terrible when we're sick.'

'I thought maybe when I got your letter,' Mrs Garden said awkwardly, 'I thought I might come in and talk to you. We haven't been married very long, Jim and I, and now when he comes back we're going to be saddled with a baby, and instead of starting out again together and going dancing and having a good time together, we're going to have responsibilities and everything. And I thought maybe you could tell me something to do.'

'Of course you did,' Mrs Hope said. 'I meet so many people,' she added, looking down at the desk. 'I don't think anyone has ever come to see me before, though.'

'They say, "Gain one, lose one,"' Mrs Garden said. 'I don't know what I'd do if anything happened to Jim.'

'Love is a very important thing,' Mrs Hope said.

'I haven't even told him yet,' Mrs Garden went on. 'Every time I write him I mean to put it in, about the baby, and then I think how awful he'll feel.'

Mrs Hope leaned back in her chair and picked up the string of beads. 'My dear,' she said, 'you would really be surprised how much trouble there is in the world. If I can do anything to make the skies brighter for any of the poor people I meet, I have served my purpose in life.'

'I thought you might just give me some advice,' Mrs Garden said. 'You were so kind that day, and I'm afraid I don't know anyone else. Not in New York, anyway, and I wanted to talk to someone.'

'And my little note comforted you?' Mrs Hope said. She smiled wistfully. 'This is the first time I have been allowed to see that I am doing some good. I talk to people everywhere and ask them for their names and addresses, and then when I feel that they need a friendly word, I send them a little note telling them to be of good heart.'

'I know,' Mrs Garden said. 'You told me, that day on the bus.'

'On buses and everywhere,' Mrs Hope said. 'I meet people wherever I go.'

'But you can help me,' Mrs Garden said, 'can't you?'

Mrs Hope smiled and put her hand on Mrs Garden's. 'Let me show you,' she said. She got up again and went over to the table by the bed. From a drawer in it she took a big scrapbook. 'I make copies of all my letters,' she said, 'so I can send more to the same people if I think they need it.' She handed the big book to Mrs Garden. Then she took the desk chair and brought it over. 'Wait till you see,' she said, taking half of the book in her lap. On the first page a slip of paper was pasted with 'A word to the wise is sufficient' written on it in Mrs Hope's careful hand. 'Here is my first letter – to a boy who wanted to change his job,' she said. 'See, here, I tell him to be careful in his decision.'

'Don't think I'm the type of person who's always complaining,' Mrs Garden said, turning to look at Mrs Hope. 'But we had so many plans for our life together.'

'This is odd,' Mrs Hope said, turning the page. 'You ought to look at this one. Here was a girl with your same situation. Let me see, what did I say to her?' She leaned forward to read the letter.

'I write to him every other day,' Mrs Garden said, 'and I have to write today. I want to have my mind made up.'

'Of course you do,' Mrs Hope said. 'This is one I

wrote to Mr Adolf Hitler. When he first started killing and rampaging, that was. I said for him to look into his heart and find love.' She touched the letter pasted on the page. 'I don't very often write like that, but some people are so much in need of a thoughtful word.'

Mrs Garden's lips trembled and she put her hand up to her mouth. 'I suppose everyone gets desperate sometimes,' she said.

'Everyone does, my dear.' Mrs Hope waited a minute, then closed the scrapbook and went over and put it carefully away in the drawer. 'You haven't eaten any candy,' she said. She took the plate and passed it to Mrs Garden, who shook her head. 'I wish I could ask you to stay for lunch,' Mrs Hope said, 'but I only have a sandwich and a cup of tea here in my room.'

'I just had breakfast,' Mrs Garden said. She stood up and picked up her pocketbook. 'It's been very nice,' she said.

'I've enjoyed seeing you again,' Mrs Hope said. 'Maybe we'll meet again on a bus sometime.'

'I hope so,' Mrs Garden said. She went toward the door.

Mrs Hope followed her. 'I can't tell you how comforting it's been,' she said, 'knowing how much good my little letters bring.'

Mrs Garden opened the door. 'I'm sure they do,' she said. 'Well, goodbye.'

'Wait a minute,' Mrs Hope said. She ran over, picked up Mrs Garden's letter from the desk, and brought it to her. 'You don't want to forget this,' she said. 'Keep it near

you, to read when things get dark. Goodbye, my dear.'
She stood courteously by the door until Mrs Garden
closed it behind her.

Outside the door, Mrs Garden waited a minute, fumbling in her pocketbook for her gloves. She heard Mrs Hope cross the room, humming softly. Then there was the movement of a chair across the floor. Straightening the room, Mrs Garden thought, pulling on a glove absentmindedly. She heard the click of the cedar beads brushing against something; probably the desk. There was silence for a minute; then Mrs Garden heard the faint scratching of Mrs Hope's pen. With only one glove on and her pocketbook flying wildly behind her, Mrs Garden turned and ran down the stairs and out into the warm noon sun.

Charles

The day my son Laurie started kindergarten he renounced corduroy overalls with bibs and began wearing blue jeans with a belt; I watched him go off the first morning with the older girl next door, seeing clearly that an era of my life was ended, my sweet-voiced nursery-school tot replaced by a long-trousered, swaggering character who forgot to stop at the corner and wave good-bye to me.

He came home the same way, the front door slamming open, his cap on the floor, and the voice suddenly become raucous shouting, 'Isn't anybody *here*?'

At lunch he spoke insolently to his father, spilled his baby sister's milk, and remarked that his teacher said we were not to take the name of the Lord in vain.

'How *was* school today?' I asked, elaborately casual.

'All right,' he said.

'Did you learn anything?' his father asked.

Laurie regarded his father coldly. 'I didn't learn nothing,' he said.

'Anything,' I said. 'Didn't learn anything.'

'The teacher spanked a boy, though,' Laurie said, addressing his bread and butter. 'For being fresh,' he added, with his mouth full.

'What did he do?' I asked. 'Who was it?'

Laurie thought. 'It was Charles,' he said. 'He was fresh. The teacher spanked him and made him stand in a corner. He was awfully fresh.'

'What did he do?' I asked again, but Laurie slid off his chair, took a cookie, and left, while his father was still saying, 'See here, young man.'

The next day Laurie remarked at lunch, as soon as he sat, down, 'Well, Charles was bad again today.' He grinned enormously and said, 'Today Charles hit the teacher.'

'Good heavens,' I said, mindful of the Lord's name, 'I suppose he got spanked again?'

'He sure did,' Laurie said. 'Look up,' he said to his father.

'What?' his father said, looking up.

'Look down,' Laurie said. 'Look at my thumb. Gee, you're dumb.' He began to laugh insanely.

'Why did Charles hit the teacher?' I asked quickly.

'Because she tried to make him color with red crayons,' Laurie said. 'Charles wanted to color with green crayons so he hit the teacher and she spanked him and said nobody play with Charles but everybody did.'

The third day – it was Wednesday of the first week –. Charles bounced a see-saw on to the head of a little girl and made her bleed, and the teacher made him stay inside all during recess. Thursday Charles had to stand in a corner during story-time because, he kept pounding his feet on the floor. Friday Charles was deprived of blackboard privileges because he threw chalk.

Charles

On Saturday I remarked to my husband, 'Do you think kindergarten is too unsettling for Laurie? All this toughness, and bad grammar, and this Charles boy sounds like such a bad influence.'

'It'll be all right,' my husband said reassuringly. 'Bound to be people like Charles in the world. Might as well meet them now as later.'

On Monday Laurie came home late, full of news. 'Charles,' he shouted as he came up the hill; I was waiting anxiously on the front steps. 'Charles,' Laurie yelled all the way up the hill, 'Charles was bad again.'

'Come right in,' I said, as soon as he came close enough. 'Lunch is waiting.'

'You know what Charles did?' he demanded, following me through the door. 'Charles yelled so in school they sent a boy in from first grade to tell the teacher she had to make Charles keep quiet, and so Charles had to stay after school. And so all the children stayed to watch him.'

'What did he do?' I asked.

'He just sat there,' Laurie said, climbing into his chair at the table. 'Hi, Pop, y'old dust mop.'

'Charles had to stay after school today,' I told my husband. 'Everyone stayed with him.'

'What does this Charles look like?' my husband asked Laurie. 'What's his other name?'

'He's bigger than me,' Laurie said. 'And he doesn't have any rubbers and he doesn't ever wear a jacket.'

Monday night was the first Parent-Teachers meeting, and only the fact that the baby had a cold kept me from going; I wanted passionately to meet Charles's mother. On Tuesday Laurie remarked suddenly, 'Our teacher had a friend come to see her in school today.'

'Charles's mother?' my husband and I asked simultaneously.

'Naaah,' Laurie said scornfully. 'It was a man who came and made us do exercises, we had to touch our toes. Look.' He climbed down from his chair and squatted down and touched his toes. 'Like this,' he said. He got solemnly back into his chair and said, picking up his fork, 'Charles didn't even *do* exercises.'

'That's fine,' I said heartily. 'Didn't Charles want to do exercises?'

'Naaah,' Laurie said. 'Charles was so fresh to the teacher's friend he wasn't *let* do exercises.'

'Fresh again?' I said.

'He kicked the teacher's friend,' Laurie said. 'The teacher's friend told Charles to touch his toes like I just did and Charles kicked him.'

'What are they going to do about Charles, do you suppose?' Laurie's father asked him.

Laurie shrugged elaborately. 'Throw him out of school, I guess,' he said.

Wednesday and Thursday were routine; Charles yelled during story hour and hit a boy in the stomach and made him cry. On Friday Charles stayed after school again and so did all the other children.

With the third week of kindergarten Charles was an institution in our family; the baby was being a Charles when she cried all afternoon; Laurie did a Charles when

Charles

he filled his wagon full of mud and pulled it through the kitchen; even my husband, when he caught his elbow in the telephone cord and pulled telephone, ashtray, and a bowl of flowers off the table, said, after the first minute, 'Looks like Charles.'

During the third and fourth weeks it looked like a reformation in Charles; Laurie reported grimly at lunch on Thursday of the third week, 'Charles was so good today the teacher gave him an apple.'

'What?' I said, and my husband added warily, 'You mean Charles?'

'Charles,' Laurie said. 'He gave the crayons around and he picked up the books afterward and the teacher said he was her helper.'

'What happened?' I asked incredulously.

'He was her helper, that's all,' Laurie said, and shrugged.

'Can this be true, about Charles?' I asked my husband that night. 'Can something like this happen?'

'Wait and see,' my husband said cynically. 'When you've got a Charles to deal with, this may mean he's only plotting.'

He seemed to be wrong. For over a week Charles was the teacher's helper; each day he handed things out and he picked things up; no one had to stay after school.

'The P.T.A. meeting's next week again,' I told my husband one evening. 'I'm going to find Charles's mother there.'

'Ask her what happened to Charles,' my husband said. 'I'd like to know.'

'I'd like to know myself,' I said.

On Friday of that week things were back to normal. 'You know what Charles did today?' Laurie demanded at the lunch table, in a voice slightly awed. 'He told a little girl to say a word and she said it and the teacher washed her mouth out with soap and Charles laughed.'

'What word?' his father asked unwisely, and Laurie said, 'I'll have to whisper it to you, it's so bad.' He got down off his chair and went around to his father. His father bent his head down and Laurie whispered joyfully. His father's eyes widened.

'Did Charles tell the little girl to say *that*?' he asked respectfully.

'She said it *twice*,' Laurie said. 'Charles told her to say it *twice*.'

'What happened to Charles?' my husband asked.

'Nothing,' Laurie said. 'He was passing out the crayons.'

Monday morning Charles abandoned the little girl and said the evil word himself three or four times, getting his mouth washed out with soap each time. He also threw chalk.

My husband came to the door with me that evening as I set out for the P.T.A. meeting. 'Invite her over for a cup of tea after the meeting,' he said. 'I want to get a look at her.'

'If only she's there,' I said prayerfully.

'She'll be there,' my husband said. 'I don't see how they could hold a P.T.A. meeting without Charles's mother.'

Charles

At the meeting I sat restlessly, scanning each comfortable matronly face, trying to determine which one hid the secret of Charles. None of them looked to me haggard enough. No one stood up in the meeting and apologized for the way her son had been acting. No one mentioned Charles.

After the meeting I identified and sought out Laurie's kindergarten teacher. She had a plate with a cup of tea and a piece of chocolate cake; I had a plate with a cup of tea and a piece of marshmallow cake. We maneuvered up to one another cautiously, and smiled.

'I've been so anxious to meet you,' I said. 'I'm Laurie's mother.'

'We're all so interested in Laurie,' she said.

'Well, he certainly likes kindergarten,' I said. 'He talks about it all the time.'

'We had a little trouble adjusting, the first week or so,' she said primly, 'but now he's a fine little helper. With occasional lapses, of course.'

'Laurie usually adjusts very quickly,' I said. 'I suppose this time it's Charles's influence.'

'Charles?'

'Yes,' I said, laughing, 'you must have your hands full in that kindergarten, with Charles.'

'Charles?' she said. 'We don't have any Charles in the kindergarten.'

Pillar of Salt

For some reason a tune was running through her head when she and her husband got on the train in New Hampshire for their trip to New York; they had not been to New York for nearly a year, but the tune was from farther back than that. It was from the days when she was fifteen or sixteen, and had never seen New York except in movies, when the city was made up, to her, of penthouses filled with Noel Coward people; when the height and speed and luxury and gaiety that made up a city like New York were confused inextricably with the dullness of being fifteen, and beauty unreachable and far in the movies.

'What *is* that tune?' she said to her husband, and hummed it. 'It's from some old movie, I think.'

'I know it,' he said, and hummed it himself. 'Can't remember the words.'

He sat back comfortably. He had hung up their coats, put the suitcases on the rack, and had taken his magazine out. 'I'll think of it sooner or later,' he said.

She looked out the window first, tasting it almost secretly, savoring the extreme pleasure of being on a moving train with nothing to do for six hours but read and nap and go into the dining-car, going farther and farther every minute from the children, from the kitchen floor, with even the hills being incredibly left behind, changing into fields and trees too far away from home to be daily. 'I love trains,' she said, and her husband nodded sympathetically into his magazine.

Two weeks ahead, two unbelievable weeks, with all arrangements made, no further planning to do, except perhaps what theatres or what restaurants. A friend with an apartment went on a convenient vacation, there was enough money in the bank to make a trip to New York compatible with new snow suits for the children; there was the smoothness of unopposed arrangements, once the initial obstacles had been overcome, as though when they had really made up their minds, nothing dared stop them. The baby's sore throat cleared up. The plumber came, finished his work in two days, and left. The dresses had been altered in time; the hardware store could be left safely, once they had found the excuse of looking over new city products. New York had not burned down, had not been quarantined, their friend had gone away according to schedule, and Brad had the keys to the apartment in his pocket. Everyone knew where to reach everyone else; there was a list of plays not to miss and a list of items to look out for in the stores – diapers, dress materials, fancy canned goods, tarnish-proof silverware boxes. And, finally, the train was there, performing its function, pacing through the afternoon, carrying them legally and with determination to New York.

Margaret looked curiously at her husband, inactive in the middle of the afternoon on a train, at the other

Pillar of Salt

fortunate people traveling, at the sunny country outside, looked again to make sure, and then opened her book. The tune was still in her head, she hummed it and heard her husband take it up softly as he turned a page in his magazine.

In the dining-car she ate roast beef, as she would have done in a restaurant at home, reluctant to change over too quickly to the new, tantalizing food of a vacation. She had ice cream for dessert but became uneasy over her coffee because they were due in New York in an hour and she still had to put on her coat and hat, relishing every gesture, and Brad must take the suitcases down and put away the magazines. They stood at the end of the car for the interminable underground run, picking up their suitcases and putting them down again, moving restlessly inch by inch.

The station was a momentary shelter, moving visitors gradually into a world of people and sound and light to prepare them for the blasting reality of the street outside. She saw it for a minute from the sidewalk before she was in a taxi moving into the middle of it, and then they were bewilderingly caught and carried on uptown and whirled out on to another sidewalk and Brad paid the taxi driver and put his head back to look up at the apartment house. 'This is it, all right,' he said, as though he had doubted the driver's ability to find a number so simply given. Upstairs in the elevator, and the key fit the door. They had never seen their friend's apartment before, but it was reasonably familiar – a friend moving from New Hampshire to New York carries private pictures of a home not erasable in a few years, and the apartment had enough of home in it to settle Brad immediately in the right chair and comfort her with instinctive trust of the linen and blankets.

'This is home for two weeks,' Brad said, and stretched. After the first few minutes they both went to the windows automatically; New York was below, as arranged, and the houses across the street were apartment houses filled with unknown people.

'It's wonderful,' she said. There were cars down there, and people, and the noise was there. 'I'm so happy,' she said, and kissed her husband.

They went sight-seeing the first day; they had breakfast in an Automat and went to the top of the Empire State building.

'Got it all fixed up now,' Brad said, at the top. 'Wonder just where that plane hit.'

They tried to peer down on all four sides, but were embarrassed about asking. 'After all,' she said reasonably, giggling in a corner, 'if something of mine got broken I wouldn't want people poking around asking to see the pieces.'

'If you owned the Empire State building you wouldn't care,' Brad said.

They traveled only in taxis the first few days, and one taxi had a door held on with a piece of string; they pointed to it and laughed silently at each other, and on about the third day, the taxi they were riding in got a flat tire on Broadway and they had to get out and find another.

Pillar of Salt

'We've only got eleven days left,' she said one day, and then, seemingly minutes later, 'we've already been here six days.'

They had got in touch with the friends they had expected to get in touch with, they were going to a Long Island summer home for a week end. 'It looks pretty dreadful right now,' their hostess said cheerfully over the phone, 'and we're leaving in a week ourselves, but I'd never *forgive* you if you didn't see it *once* while you were here.' The weather had been fair but cool, with a definite autumn awareness, and the clothes in the store windows were dark and already hinting at furs and velvets. She wore her coat every day, and suits most of the time. The light dresses she had brought were hanging in the closet in the apartment, and she was thinking now of getting a sweater in one of the big stores, something impractical for New Hampshire, but probably good for Long Island.

'I have to do some shopping, at least one day,' she said to Brad, and he groaned.

'Don't ask me to carry packages,' he said.

'You aren't up to a good day's shopping,' she told him, 'not after all this walking around you've been doing. Why don't you go to a movie or something?'

'I want to do some shopping myself,' he said mysteriously. Perhaps he was talking about her Christmas present; she had thought vaguely of getting such things done in New York; the children would be pleased with novelties from the city, toys not seen in their home stores. At any rate she said, 'You'll probably be able to get to your wholesalers at last.'

They were on their way to visit another friend, who had found a place to live by a miracle and warned them consequently not to quarrel with the appearance of the building, or the stairs, or the neighborhood. All three were bad, and the stairs were three flights, narrow and dark, but there was a place to live at the top. Their friend had not been in New York long, but he lived by himself in two rooms, and had easily caught the mania for slim tables and low bookcases which made his rooms look too large for the furniture in some places, too cramped and uncomfortable in others.

'What a lovely place,' she said when she came in, and then was sorry when her host said, 'Some day this damn situation will let up and I'll be able to settle down in a really decent place.'

There were other people there; they sat and talked companionably about the same subjects then current in New Hampshire, but they drank more than they would have at home and it left them strangely unaffected; their voices were louder and their words more extravagant; their gestures, on the other hand, were smaller, and they moved a finger where in New Hampshire they would have waved an arm. Margaret said frequently, 'We're just staying here for a couple of weeks, on a vacation,' and she said, 'It's wonderful, so *exciting*,' and she said, 'We were *terribly* lucky; this friend went out of town just at the right . . .'

Finally the room was very full and noisy, and she went into a corner near a window to catch her breath. The window had been opened and shut all evening, depending on whether the person standing next to it had both hands free; and now it was shut, with the clear sky outside. Someone came and stood next to her, and she said, 'Listen to the noise outside. It's as bad as it is inside.'

He said, 'In a neighborhood like this someone's always getting killed.'

She frowned. 'It sounds different than before. I mean, there's a different sound to it.'

'Alcoholics,' he said. 'Drunks in the streets. Fighting going on across the way.' He wandered away, carrying his drink.

She opened the window and leaned out, and there were people hanging out of the windows across the way shouting, and people standing in the street looking up and shouting, and from across the way she heard clearly, 'Lady, lady.' They must mean me, she thought, they're all looking this way. She leaned out farther and the voices shouted incoherently but somehow making an audible whole, 'Lady, your house is on fire, lady, lady.'

She closed the window firmly and turned around to the other people in the room, raising her voice a little. 'Listen,' she said, 'they're saying the house is on fire.' She was desperately afraid of their laughing at her, of looking like a fool while Brad across the room looked at her blushing. She said again, 'The *house* is on *fire*,' and added, 'They say,' for fear of sounding too vehement. The people nearest to her turned and someone said, 'She says the house is on fire.'

She wanted to get to Brad and couldn't see him; her host was not in sight either, and the people all around were strangers. They don't listen to me, she thought, I might as well not be here, and she went to the outside door and opened it. There was no smoke, no flame, but she was telling herself, I might as well not be here, so she abandoned Brad in panic and ran without her hat and coat down the stairs, carrying a glass in one hand and a package of matches in the other. The stairs were insanely long, but they were clear and safe, and she opened the street door and ran out. A man caught her arm and said, 'Everyone out of the house?' and she said, 'No, Brad's still there.' The fire engines swept around the corner, with people leaning out of the windows watching them, and the man holding her arm said, 'It's down here,' and left her. The fire was two houses away; they could see flames behind the top windows, and smoke against the night sky, but in ten minutes it was finished and the fire engines pulled away with an air of martyrdom for hauling out all their equipment to put out a ten-minute fire.

She went back upstairs slowly and with embarrassment, and found Brad and took him home.

'I was so frightened,' she said to him when they were safely in bed, 'I lost my head completely.'

'You should have tried to find someone,' he said.

'They wouldn't listen,' she insisted. 'I kept telling them and they wouldn't listen and then I thought I must have been mistaken. I had some idea of going down to see what was going on.'

'Lucky it was no worse,' Brad said sleepily.

'I felt trapped,' she said. 'High up in that old building with a fire; it's like a nightmare. And in a strange city.'

Pillar of Salt

'Well, it's all over now,' Brad said.

The same faint feeling of insecurity tagged her the next day; she went shopping alone and Brad went off to see hardware, after all. She got on a bus to go downtown and the bus was too full to move when it came time for her to get out. Wedged standing in the aisle she said, 'Out, please,' and, 'Excuse me,' and by the time she was loose and near the door the bus had started again and she got off a stop beyond. 'No one *listens* to me,' she said to herself. 'Maybe it's because I'm too polite.' In the stores the prices were all too high and the sweaters looked disarmingly like New Hampshire ones. The toys for the children filled her with dismay; they were so obviously for New York children: hideous little parodies of adult life, cash registers, tiny pushcarts with imitation fruit, telephones that really worked (as if there weren't enough phones in New York that really worked), miniature milk bottles in a carrying case. 'We get our milk from cows,' Margaret told the salesgirl. 'My children wouldn't know what these were.' She was exaggerating, and felt guilty for a minute, but no one was around to catch her.

She had a picture of small children in the city dressed like their parents, following along with a miniature mechanical civilization, toy cash registers in larger and larger sizes that eased them into the real thing, millions of clattering jerking small imitations that prepared them nicely for taking over the large useless toys their parents lived by. She bought a pair of skis for her son, which she knew would be inadequate for the New Hampshire snow, and a wagon for her daughter inferior to the one Brad could make at home in an hour. Ignoring the toy mailboxes, the small phonographs with special small records, the kiddie cosmetics, she left the store and started home.

She was frankly afraid by now to take a bus; she stood on the corner and waited for a taxi. Glancing down at her feet, she saw a dime on the sidewalk and tried to pick it up, but there were too many people for her to bend down, and she was afraid to shove to make room for fear of being stared at. She put her foot on the dime and then saw a quarter near it, and a nickel. Someone dropped a pocketbook, she thought, and put her other foot on the quarter, stepping quickly to make it look natural; then she saw another dime and another nickel, and a third dime in the gutter. People were passing her, back and forth, all the time, rushing, pushing against her, not looking at her, and she was afraid to get down and start gathering up the money. Other people saw it and went past, and she realized that no one was going to pick it up. They were all embarrassed, or in too much of a hurry, or too crowded. A taxi stopped to let someone off, and she hailed it. She lifted her feet off the dime and the quarter, and left them there when she got into the taxi. This taxi went slowly and bumped as it went; she had begun to notice that the gradual decay was not peculiar to the taxis. The buses were cracking open in unimportant seams, the leather seats broken and stained. The buildings were going, too – in one of the nicest stores there had been a great gaping hole in

Pillar of Salt

the tiled foyer, and you walked around it. Corners of the buildings seemed to be crumbling away into fine dust that drifted downward, the granite was eroding unnoticed. Every window she saw on her way uptown seemed to be broken; perhaps every street corner was peppered with small change. The people were moving faster than ever before; a girl in a red hat appeared at the upper side of the taxi window and was gone beyond the lower side before you could see the hat; store windows were so terribly bright because you only caught them for a fraction of a second. The people seemed hurled on in a frantic action that made every hour forty-five minutes long, every day nine hours, every year fourteen days. Food was so elusively fast, eaten in such a hurry, that you were always hungry, always speeding to a new meal with new people. Everything was imperceptibly quicker every minute. She stepped into the taxi on one side and stepped out the other side at her home; she pressed the fifth-floor button on the elevator and was coming down again, bathed and dressed and ready for dinner with Brad. They went out for dinner and were coming in again, hungry and hurrying to bed in order to get to breakfast with lunch beyond. They had been in New York nine days; tomorrow was Saturday and they were going to Long Island, coming home Sunday, and then Wednesday they were going home, really home. By the time she had thought of it they were on the train to Long Island; the train was broken, the seats torn and the floor dirty; one of the doors wouldn't open and the windows wouldn't shut. Passing through the outskirts of the city, she thought, It's as though everything were traveling so fast that the solid stuff couldn't stand it and were going to pieces under the strain, cornices blowing off and windows caving in. She knew she was afraid to say it truly, afraid to face the knowledge that it was a voluntary neck-breaking speed, a deliberate whirling faster and faster to end in destruction.

On Long Island, their hostess led them into a new piece of New York, a house filled with New York furniture as though on rubber bands, pulled this far, stretched taut, and ready to snap back to the city; to an apartment, as soon as the door was opened and the lease, fully paid, had expired. 'We've had this place every year for simply ages,' their hostess said. 'Otherwise we couldn't have gotten it *possibly* this year.'

'It's an awfully nice place,' Brad said. 'I'm surprised you don't live here all year round.'

'Got to get back to the city *some* time,' their hostess said, and laughed.

'Not much like New Hampshire,' Brad said. He was beginning to be a little homesick, Margaret thought; he wants to yell, just once. Since the fire scare she was apprehensive about large groups of people gathering together; when friends began to drop in after dinner she waited for a while, telling herself they were on the ground floor, she could run right outside, all the windows were open; then she excused herself and went to bed. When Brad came to bed much later she woke up and he said irritably, 'We've been playing anagrams. Such

Pillar of Salt

crazy people.' She said sleepily, 'Did you win?' and fell asleep before he told her.

The next morning she and Brad went for a walk while their host and hostess read the Sunday papers. 'If you turn to the right outside the door,' their hostess said encouragingly, 'and walk about three blocks down, you'll come to our beach.'

'What do they want with our beach?' their host said. 'It's too damn cold to do anything down there.'

'They can look at the *water*,' their hostess said.

They walked down to the beach; at this time of year it was bare and windswept, yet still nodding hideously under traces of its summer plumage, as though it thought itself warmly inviting. There were occupied houses on the way there, for instance, and a lonely lunchstand was open, bravely advertising hot dogs and root beer. The man in the lunchstand watched them go by, his face cold and unsympathetic. They walked far past him, out of sight of houses, on to a stretch of grey pebbled sand that lay between the grey water on one side and the grey pebbled sand dunes on the other.

'Imagine going swimming here,' she said with a shiver. The beach pleased her; it was oddly familiar and reassuring and at the same time that she realized this, the little tune came back to her, bringing a double recollection. The beach was the one where she had lived in imagination, writing for herself dreary love-broken stories where the heroine walked beside the wild waves; the little tune was the symbol of the golden world she escaped into to avoid the everyday dreariness that drove her into writing depressing stories about the beach. She laughed out loud and Brad said, 'What on earth's so funny about his God-forsaken landscape?'

'I was just thinking how far away from the city it seems,' she said falsely.

The sky and the water and the sand were grey enough to make it feel like late afternoon instead of midmorning; she was tired and wanted to go back, but Brad said suddenly, 'Look at that,' and she turned and saw a girl running down over the dunes, carrying her hat, and her hair flying behind her.

'Only way to get warm on a day like this,' Brad remarked, but Margaret said, 'She looks frightened.'

The girl saw them and came toward them, slowing down as she approached them. She was eager to reach them but when she came within speaking distance the familiar embarrassment, the not wanting to look like a fool, made her hesitate and look from one to the other of them uncomfortably.

'Do you know where I can find a policeman?' she asked finally.

Brad looked up and down the bare rocky beach and said solemnly, 'There don't seem to be any around. Is there something we can do?'

'I don't think so,' the girl said. 'I really need a policeman.'

They go to the police for everything, Margaret thought, these people, these New York people, it's as though they had selected a section of the population to act as problem-solvers, and so no matter what they want they look for a policeman.

'Be glad to help you if we can,' Brad said.

The girl hesitated again. 'Well, if you *must* know,' she said crossly, 'there's a leg up there.'

They waited politely for the girl to explain, but she only said, 'Come *on*, then,' and waved to them to follow her. She led them over the dunes to a spot near a small inlet, where the dunes gave way abruptly to an intruding head of water. A leg was lying on the sand near the water, and the girl gestured at it and said, 'There,' as though it were her own property and they had insisted on having a share.

They walked over to it and Brad bent down gingerly. 'It's a leg all right,' he said. It looked like part of a wax dummy, a death-white wax leg neatly cut off at top-thigh and again just above the ankle, bent comfortably at the knee and resting on the sand. 'It's real,' Brad said, his voice slightly different. 'You're right about that policeman.'

They walked together to the lunchstand and the man listened unenthusiastically while Brad called the police. When the police came they all walked out again to where the leg was lying and Brad gave the police their names and addresses, and then said, 'Is it all right to go on home?'

'What the hell you want to hang around for?' the policeman inquired with heavy humor. 'You waiting for the rest of him?'

They went back to their host and hostess, talking

about the leg, and their host apologized, as though he had been guilty of a breach of taste in allowing his guests to come on a human leg; their hostess said with interest, 'There was an arm washed up in Bensonhurst, I've been reading about it.'

'One of these killings,' the host said.

Upstairs Margaret said abruptly, 'I suppose it starts to happen first in the suburbs,' and when Brad said, 'What starts to happen?' she said hysterically, 'People starting to come apart.'

In order to reassure their host and hostess about their minding the leg, they stayed until the last afternoon train to New York. Back in their apartment again it seemed to Margaret that the marble in the house lobby had begun to age a little; even in two days there were new perceptible cracks. The elevator seemed a little rusty, and there was a fine film of dust over everything in the apartment. They went to bed feeling uncomfortable, and the next morning Margaret said immediately, 'I'm going to stay in today.'

'You're not upset about yesterday, are you?'

'Not a bit,' Margaret said. 'I just want to stay in and rest.'

After some discussion Brad decided to go off again by himself; he still had people it was important to see and places he must go in the few days they had left. After breakfast in the Automat Margaret came back alone to the apartment, carrying the mystery story she had bought on the way. She hung up her coat and hat and sat down by the window with the noise and the people far below, looking out at the sky where it was grey beyond the houses across the street.

Pillar of Salt

I'm not going to worry about it, she said to herself, no sense thinking all the time about things like that, spoil your vacation and Brad's too. No sense worrying, people get ideas like that and then worry about them.

The nasty little tune was running through her head again, with its burden of suavity and expensive perfume. The houses across the street were silent and perhaps unoccupied at this time of day; she let her eyes move with the rhythm of the tune, from window to window along one floor. By gliding quickly across two windows, she could make one line of the tune fit one floor of windows, and then a quick breath and a drop down to the next floor; it had the same number of windows and the tune had the same number of beats, and then the next floor and the next. She stopped suddenly when it seemed to her that the windowsill she had just passed had soundlessly crumpled and fallen into fine sand; when she looked back it was there as before but then it seemed to be the windowsill above and to the right, and finally a corner of the roof.

No sense worrying, she told herself, forcing her eyes down to the street, stop thinking about things all the time. Looking down at the street for long made her dizzy and she stood up and went into the small bedroom of the apartment. She had made the bed before going out to breakfast, like any good housewife, but now she deliberately took it apart, stripping the blankets and sheets off one by one, and then she made it again, taking a long time over the corners and smoothing out every wrinkle. '*That's* done,' she said when she was through, and went back to the window. When she looked across the street the tune started again, window to window, sills dissolving and falling downward. She leaned forward and looked down at her own window, something she had never thought of before, down to the sill. It was partly eaten away; when she touched the stone a few crumbs rolled off and fell.

It was eleven o'clock; Brad was looking at blowtorches by now and would not be back before one, if even then. She thought of writing a letter home, but the impulse left her before she found paper and pen. Then it occurred to her that she might take a nap, a thing she had never done in the morning in her life, and she went in and lay down on the bed. Lying down, she felt the building shaking.

No sense worrying, she told herself again, as though it were a charm against witches, and got up and found her coat and hat and put them on. I'll just get some cigarettes and some letter paper, she thought, just run down to the corner. Panic caught her going down in the elevator; it went too fast, and when she stepped out in the lobby it was only the people standing around who kept her from running. As it was, she went quickly out of the building and into the street. For a minute she hesitated, wanting to go back. The cars were going past so rapidly, the people hurrying as always, but the panic of the elevator drove her on finally. She went to the corner, and, following the people flying along ahead, ran out into the street, to hear a horn almost overhead and a shout from behind her, and the noise of brakes. She ran blindly

Pillar of Salt

on and reached the other side where she stopped and looked around. The truck was going on its appointed way around the corner, the people going past on either side of her, parting to go around her where she stood.

No one even noticed me, she thought with reassurance, everyone who saw me has gone by long ago. She went into the drugstore ahead of her and asked the man for cigarettes; the apartment now seemed safer to her than the street – she could walk up the stairs. Coming out of the store and walking to the corner, she kept as close to the buildings as possible, refusing to give way to the rightful traffic coming out of the doorways. On the corner she looked carefully at the light; it was green, but it looked as though it were going to change. Always safer to wait, she thought, don't want to walk into another track.

People pushed past her and some were caught in the middle of the street when the light changed. One woman, more cowardly than the rest, turned and ran back to the curb, but the others stood in the middle of the street, leaning forward and then backward according to the traffic moving past them on both sides. One got to the farther curb in a brief break in the line of cars, the others were a fraction of a second too late and waited. Then the light changed again and as the cars slowed down Margaret put a foot on the street to go, but a taxi swinging wildly around her corner frightened her back and she stood on the curb again. By the time the taxi had gone the light was due to change again and she thought, I can wait once more, no sense getting caught out in the middle. A man beside her tapped his foot impatiently for the light to change back; two girls came past her and walked out into the street a few steps to wait, moving back a little when cars came too close, talking busily all the time. I ought to stay right with them, Margaret thought, but then they moved back against her and the light changed and the man next to her charged into the street and the two girls in front waited a minute and then moved slowly on, still talking, and Margaret started to follow and then decided to wait. A crowd of people formed around her suddenly; they had come off a bus and were crossing here, and she had a sudden feeling of being jammed in the center and forced out into the street when all of them moved as one with the light changing, and she elbowed her way desperately out of the crowd and went off to lean against a building and wait. It seemed to her that people passing were beginning to look at her. What do they think of me, she wondered, and stood up straight as though she were waiting for someone. She looked at her watch and frowned, and then thought, What a fool I must look like, no one here ever saw me before, they all go by too fast. She went back to the curb again but the green light was just changing to red and she thought, I'll go back to the drugstore and have a coke, no sense going back to that apartment.

The man looked at her unsurprised in the drugstore and she sat and ordered a coke but suddenly as she was drinking it the panic caught her again and she thought of the people who had been with her when she first started to cross the street, blocks away by now, having tried and made perhaps a dozen lights while she had hesitated at the first; people by now a mile or so downtown, because they had been going steadily while she had been trying to gather her courage. She paid the man quickly, restrained an impulse to say that there was nothing wrong with the coke, she just had to get back, that was all, and she hurried down to the corner again.

The minute the light changes, she told herself firmly; there's no sense. The light changed before she was ready and in the minute before she collected herself traffic turning the corner overwhelmed her and she shrank back against the curb. She looked longingly at the cigar store on the opposite corner, with her apartment house beyond; she wondered, How do people ever manage to get there, and knew that by wondering, by admitting a doubt, she was lost. The light changed and she looked at it with hatred, a dumb thing, turning back and forth, back and forth, with no purpose and no meaning. Looking to either side of her slyly, to see if anyone were watching, she stepped quietly backward, one step, two, until she was well away from the curb. Back in the drugstore again she waited for some sign of recognition from the clerk and saw none; he regarded her with the same apathy as he had the first time. He gestured without interest at the telephone; he doesn't care, she thought, it doesn't matter to him who I call.

She had no time to feel like a fool, because they answered the phone immediately and agreeably and found him right away. When he answered the phone, his voice sounding surprised and matter-of-fact, he could only say miserably, 'I'm in the drugstore on the corner. Come and get me.'

'What's the matter?' He was not anxious to come.

'Please come and get me,' she said into the black mouthpiece that might or might not tell him, 'please come and get me, Brad. *Please.*'

Murder on Miss Lederer's Birthday

From the kitchenette where Miss Alliston was making breakfast came the pleasant sound of coffee percolating and the rather flat sound of Miss Alliston humming cheerfully to herself. It was not quite nine o'clock, and the sunlight had just begun to creep along the edge of the living room carpet; a breeze came gently through the half-opened window and stirred the petals of the geranium on the windowsill. It was an apartment clearly inhabited by two maiden ladies of a certain age; an unashamed rocking chair sat next to the radiator, with a tiny needlepoint footstool in front of it; on the mantel were two matched earthenware jugs, each saying SOUVENIR OF MEXICO CITY; all the chairs were daintily antimacassared. As though extremely conscious of the fact that he was a spot of local color, a large gray tomcat sat washing his face in the patch of sunlight on the floor.

Miss Alliston and Miss Lederer were schoolteachers ('the Two Musketeers of Houston High,' they called themselves privately, and they were given to wildly reckless dinners at Italian restaurants on Friday afternoons, with half a bottle of red wine and veal scallopine), and they had done their best to make their apartment homey. 'I feel so sorry for those other poor girls,' they were fond of observing to each other, 'living in furnished rooms or private homes, with none of our comfort, and none of our . . . well, dear . . . *freedom.*'

Miss Alliston was the senior by a year and a half; at forty-one, she'd given herself the position of leader. It had been Miss Alliston's idea to go to Mexico one summer. It was to Miss Alliston, too, that the one souvenir ashtray belonged; she enjoyed an occasional cigarette after their Friday evening meal, although she disapproved of the habit for Miss Lederer. 'I do so enjoy my smokes,' she would say sinfully, 'but no one recognizes more clearly than I how filthy a habit it is.'

Miss Alliston and Miss Lederer took turns on Saturday mornings getting up and making breakfast. This morning, Miss Alliston was unusually cheerful, for it was Miss Lederer's birthday and they had planned An Occasion. This morning they were going to the Museum of Modern Art, and in the afternoon to a theater matinee. The matinee was Miss Alliston's treat, a birthday present for her friend.

Miss Alliston took the cinnamon buns from the oven and put them on the table. Then, taking off her apron and hanging it on the hook on the door to the kitchenette, she went into the bedroom.

'Paula,' she cried gaily, 'top of the morning to you! And happy birthday!'

Miss Lederer stirred and opened her eyes. 'Thank you, Evelyn,' she murmured. Miss Alliston began to sing, 'Lazy Paula, will you get up, will you get up; will you get up . . .'

Murder on Miss Lederer's Birthday

Lazy Paula sat up in bed and sniffed. 'Evelyn, weren't you sweet to make breakfast,' she said. (She had said it every time Miss Alliston had made breakfast since they'd been living together. On alternate Saturdays Miss Alliston woke up and said: 'Paula, you dear girl! Did you really make breakfast for me?')

'Come right away,' Miss Alliston said, 'or everything will get cold.'

Miss Alliston threw Miss Lederer's housecoat onto the bed and went back to fuss over the table. In a moment, Miss Lederer joined her, and the two of them sat down. Immediately the big gray cat leaped onto Miss Lederer's lap, poking his head over the edge of the table experimentally.

'Good morning, dear,' Miss Lederer said gaily to the cat. She broke off a tiny piece of cinnamon bun and held it out to the cat.

'Paula, you crazy girl,' Miss Alliston said. 'Anyway, he had his milk hours ago.' There was a sound at the apartment door. 'There's the paper,' Miss Alliston added. 'I'll get it. You sit still and finish your birthday breakfast.'

Miss Alliston opened the door and picked up the paper. 'What are the headlines, Evelyn?' Miss Lederer asked, pouring herself a second, and extravagant, cup of coffee.

'All about the war,' Miss Alliston replied, reading the paper as she closed the door behind her and started back to the table. 'The Russians are doing just marvelously, and there's good news from Africa, and

Congress has done something or other . . . We'll go over it all later.'

Both Miss Alliston and Miss Lederer were intensely interested in national and international affairs. They held heated discussions over political developments and had bought themselves a small mounted map on which they earnestly and devotedly plotted the campaigns of the war, with a good deal of disagreement and spectacular generalship. After the arrival of the morning paper, however, the world and the map had always to wait upon an enthusiastic survey of advertisements, particularly for household novelties, book sales (which they never attended), and news of prime importance, which was society, gossip, and murder. There was a murder this morning on the second page.

'My dear,' Miss Alliston gasped as she turned the page, 'such a ghastly affair!'

Miss Lederer went to stand next to Miss Alliston while they read the story.

'And attacked her!' Miss Lederer whispered, her hand to her lips. 'How fearful!'

'Horrible,' Miss Alliston confirmed, sitting back in her chair at the table with the paper.

'Read it all to me,' Miss Lederer said.

'There's no more than this,' Miss Alliston said, turning the pages haphazardly.

'Let me see if I've got it straight,' Miss Lederer said. 'This girl –'

'Alice January, her name was,' Miss Alliston added, referring to the paper. 'A dancer, a modern dancer.'

Murder on Miss Lederer's Birthday

'I'm not surprised,' Miss Lederer said, nodding, 'the way they live. And you say she was found in her apartment?'

'Her *luxurious* apartment, in Gramcrcy Park.'

Miss Lederer shuddered.

'My dear,' Miss Alliston said, leaning over the table, 'aren't you *glad* I insisted that we live in the Village?'

Miss Lederer smiled gratefully at her friend. 'Who found the body?'

'"Miss January had retired early,"' Miss Alliston read, '"telling the clerk at the switchboard she did not wish to be disturbed."'

'That's exactly what I was wondering, Evelyn,' Miss Lederer said significantly. '*Why* did she say she didn't want to be disturbed?' There was a silence as they regarded each other. Then: 'I do believe you're right,' Miss Alliston said, nodding. 'There's certainly more to it than meets the eye.'

'Exactly,' Miss Lederer said, 'Read me the rest.'

Miss Alliston consulted the paper again. '"Her body was found by the manager. She had left word to be called at eleven o'clock in the morning, and when there was no answer to the bell he opened the door with a skeleton key, and found her lying naked in the bedroom, with thirty-one stab wounds." Thirty-one stab wounds!' she repeated. 'Dreadful! Well, he locked the door again . . .'

'There's another thing,' Miss Lederer interrupted. 'What was *he* doing with a key?'

Miss Alliston looked dubious. 'Well, managers always

have keys for all the doors. To let plumbers in, and painters, and deliveries, and things like that.'

'Gracious!' Miss Lederer said. 'I'm glad no one has a key to *our* home!'

'Anyway, they say she was practically . . .' Miss Alliston fanned herself with her napkin. 'Heavens, I can't read it, Paula.'

Miss Lederer took the paper and found Miss Alliston's place. '"Dismembered,"' she read. 'I don't blame you a bit for feeling faint, Evelyn. Shall I get you a glass of water?'

'No,' Miss Alliston said, recovering slightly. 'Just don't read any more of the horrible part.'

'Well,' Miss Lederer read on, 'it seems the police are looking for "a man who was a frequent visitor to Miss January's apartment, whom she described as her manager, and a woman who is generally supposed to be a near relative of Miss January's, an elderly woman, probably an aunt."'

'No more an aunt than I am!' said Miss Alliston vehemently.

'"She was only wearing,"' Miss Lederer went on, breathlessly absorbed, '"a pearl necklace –"' Oh, my dear, imagine, a pearl necklace on the money those dancers get! And then coming to an end like that, all hacked up.'

'And attacked,' Miss Alliston said.

'"Sexually assaulted,"' Miss Lederer read from the paper. She looked up. '"No one has been arrested as yet,"' she said.

'If we pick up an afternoon paper on our way uptown,'

Murder on Miss Lederer's Birthday

Miss Alliston said, 'we might find out if there are any developments, whether the murderer has been caught, or anything.'

'I'm interested in this man she said was her manager,' Miss Lederer mused.

Miss Alliston looked at her watch. 'Good heavens! Half past ten. Paula, do you know we've been sitting here chatting for more than an hour?'

'We'll never get to the museum at this rate,' Miss Lederer said, not moving.

'The museum.' Miss Alliston's voice was rather flat. 'We won't have much time there now, will we?'

'Evelyn,' Miss Lederer said hesitantly, 'do you think we really *ought* to try and crowd the museum and a matinee all into one day? I'm not too enthusiastic about just rushing through the museum, frankly.'

'But, Paula, it's your birthday, and I don't want you to stay home because you think I don't want to go.'

'Well, I'm not too enthusiastic about just rushing through,' Miss Lederer repeated, 'but if you'd like to, I'm perfectly willing to go.'

'Well, personally, I'd really much rather just take my time and get to the matinee good and early.'

'I'm so glad, Evelyn, because I really *was* a little tired and didn't like to say so, because I knew you were counting on it.'

'If you're *sure* you don't mind not going,' Miss Alliston said.

'But we mustn't miss the matinee,' Miss Lederer said firmly.

'We certainly will not miss the matinee,' Miss Alliston confirmed. They smiled at each other proudly. 'Suppose I just run downstairs now,' Miss Alliston proposed, 'and see if any afternoon papers have come out yet.'

Miss Lederer laughed. 'You know,' she confessed, 'I'm surprised at myself, really I am. Letting myself get so interested in a sordid murder, I mean. It isn't *like* me, you know.'

Miss Alliston said, 'Well, this one interested me, especially because it took place so near here.'

'I mean, I'm not one of those persons who insist on visiting the scene of a crime, or anything,' Miss Lederer insisted.

'I would never dream of going near the scene of a crime,' Miss Alliston said with dignity. 'As it happens, however, this January murder was in a neighborhood I know slightly.'

'Really, Evelyn?'

'I used to visit friends in the vicinity,' Miss Alliston said, 'but that was many years ago, naturally.'

'You didn't ever know *her*, did you?'

'Alice? Certainly not!' Miss Alliston shook her head doubtfully. 'I may have met her, Paula, you know; I can't be sure. Perhaps I was introduced to her at one time. You know how it is with people you meet.' She got up and went into the bedroom. Miss Lederer began to reread the account in the paper.

'Dear, are you absolutely sure you don't mind about the museum?' Miss Alliston called from the bedroom.

'Absolutely,' Miss Lederer said. 'You know, I can't

Murder on Miss Lederer's Birthday

help feeling there ought to be some clues, fingerprints or something.'

Miss Alliston returned with her coat on, and stood by the table snapping and unsnapping the fastener of her pocketbook. Finally she said, 'Paula, why don't you just make another pot of coffee while I'm gone?'

'Do you really think we should?'

Miss Alliston, was brisk. 'Yes. We'll do without coffee some morning toward the end of the month, that's all. We are certainly entitled to our small pleasures, especially on your birthday.' She moved to the window and looked out. 'Such a lovely day; I wonder if we're not silly to spend it cooped up in a theater instead of out of doors.'

Miss Lederer looked up. 'You know, Evelyn, if you wanted to change the tickets for some other day, I wouldn't mind at all. Of course it's not my place to say anything, since it's your treat, but somehow the prospect of a stuffy theater . . .'

'I just don't feel in the mood for a play today, I guess,' Miss Alliston said. 'They're holding our tickets at the box office; I'll just call the theater.'

'Get the papers after you do everything else, and then you'll probably get a later edition,' Miss Lederer suggested. Miss Alliton, walking quickly, let the door slain behind her.

Miss Lederer started clearing the dishes off the table. She had the new pot of coffee percolating cheerfully when Miss Alliston returned, arms full of packages.

'It's really *dreadfully* chilly out, dear,' Miss Alliston

said 'You've no idea how wise we are to cancel our plans today.'

'Did you get the papers?' Miss Lederer asked.

Miss Alliston put the packages down. 'All the papers,' she said, 'and some potato salad and two codfish cakes and some rye bread, and, Paula, a tiny little bottle of Chianti! And I got myself a pack of cigarettes, too; the man said they were a very popular brand.'

'Good for you,' Miss Lederer said heartily. 'You deserve a little treat after being so generous about giving up the matinee.' She took the coffeepot from the stove and stood it on the table next to the two fresh cups, then sat down. The big gray cat leaped up on her lap, and she petted him. Then she selected a tabloid from the pile of papers Miss Alliston had brought and turned to the story of the murder.

Miss Alliston took her packages into the kitchen, then returned and sat down in her own place at the table. She opened her new pack of cigarettes carefully, lit one, and put it down beside her in the clean ashtray. Then she poured herself a cup of coffee and sat back comfortably.

'I saw in the headlines,' she said, 'that they've found a new secret clue.' She picked up her cigarette and puffed vigorously. 'Paula,' she continued through the smoke, 'you know, I don't think it would do any harm if we went out later for a short constitutional, and just ran over to Gramercy Park for a minute to see what we could see –'

Louisa, Please Come Home

'Louisa,' my mother's voice came over the radio; it frightened me badly for a minute. 'Louisa,' she said, 'please come home. It's been three long long years since we saw you last; Louisa, I promise you that everything will be all right. We all miss you so. We want you back again. Louisa, please come home.'

Once a year. On the anniversary of the day I ran away. Each time I heard it I was frightened again, because between one year and the next I would forget what my mother's voice sounded like, so soft and yet strange with that pleading note. I listened every year. I read the stories in the newspapers – 'Louisa Tether vanished one year ago' – or two years ago, or, three; I used to wait for the twentieth of June as though it were my birthday. I kept all the clippings at first, but secretly; with my picture on all the front pages I would have looked kind of strange if anyone had seen me cutting it out. Chandler, where I was hiding, was close enough to my old home so that the papers made a big fuss about all of it, but of course the reason I picked Chandler in the first place was because it was a big enough city for me to hide in.

I didn't just up and leave on the spur of the moment,

you know. I always knew that I was going to run away sooner or later, and I had made plans ahead of time, for whenever I decided to go. Everything had to go right the first time, because they don't usually give you a second chance on that kind of thing and anyway if it had gone wrong I would have looked like an awful fool, and my sister Carol was never one for letting people forget it when they made fools of themselves. I admit I planned it for the day before Carol's wedding on purpose, and for a long time afterward I used to try and imagine Carol's face when she finally realized that my running away was going to leave her one bridesmaid short. The papers said that the wedding went ahead as scheduled, though, and Carol told one newspaper reporter that her sister Louisa would have wanted it that way; 'She would never have meant to spoil my wedding,' Carol said, knowing perfectly well that that would be exactly what I'd meant. I'm pretty sure that the first thing Carol did when they knew I was missing was go and count the wedding presents to see what I'd taken with me.

Anyway, Carol's wedding may have been fouled up, but *my* plans went fine – better, as a matter of fact, than I had ever expected. Everyone was hurrying around the house putting up flowers and asking each other if the wedding gown had been delivered, and opening up cases of champagne and wondering what they were going to do if it rained and they couldn't use the garden, and I just closed the front door behind me and started off. There was only one bad minute when Paul saw me;

Paul has always lived next door and Carol hates him worse than she does me. My mother always used to say that every time I did something to make the family ashamed of me Paul was sure to be in it somewhere. For a long time they thought he had something to do with my running away, even though he told over and over again how hard I tried to duck away from him that afternoon when he met me going down the driveway. The papers kept calling him 'a close friend of the family', which must have overjoyed my mother, and saying that he was being questioned about possible clues to my whereabouts. Of course he never even knew that I was running away; I told him just what I told my mother before I left – that I was going to get away from all the confusion and excitement for a while; I was going downtown and would probably have a sandwich somewhere for supper and go to a movie. He bothered me for a minute there, because of course he wanted to come too. I hadn't meant to take the bus right there on the corner but with Paul tagging after me and wanting me to wait while he got the car so we could drive out and have dinner at the Inn, I had to get away fast on the first thing that came along, so I just ran for the bus and left Paul standing there; that was the only part of my plan I had to change.

I took the bus all the way downtown, although my first plan had been to walk. It turned out much better, actually, since it didn't matter at all if anyone saw me on the bus going downtown in my own home town, and I managed to get an earlier train out. I bought a round-trip ticket; that was important, because it would make them think I was coming back; that was always the way they thought about things. If you did something you had to have a reason for it, because my mother and my father and Carol never did anything unless *they* had a reason for it, so if I bought a round-trip ticket the only possible reason would be that I was coming back. Besides, if they thought I was coming back they would not be frightened so quickly and I might have more time to hide before they came looking for me. As it happened, Carol found out I was gone that same night when she couldn't sleep and came into my room for some aspirin, so at the time I had less of a head start than I thought.

I knew that they would find out about my buying the ticket; I was not silly enough to suppose that I could steal off and not leave any traces. All my plans were based on the fact that the people who get caught are the ones who attract attention by doing something strange or noticeable, and what I intended all along was to fade into some background where they would never see me. I knew they would find out about the round-trip ticket, because it was an odd thing to do in a town where you've lived all your life, but it was the last unusual thing I did. I thought when I bought it that knowing about that round-trip ticket would be some consolation to my mother and father. They would know that no matter how long I stayed away at least I always had a ticket home. I did keep the return-trip ticket quite a while, as a matter of fact. I used to carry it in my wallet as a kind of lucky charm.

Louisa, Please Come Home

I followed everything in the papers. Mrs Peacock and I used to read them at the breakfast table over our second cup of coffee before I went off to work.

'What do you think about this girl disappeared over in Rockville?' Mrs Peacock would say to me, and I'd shake my head sorrowfully and say that a girl must be really crazy to leave a handsome, luxurious home like that, or that I had kind of a notion that maybe she didn't leave at all – maybe the family had her locked up somewhere because she was a homicidal maniac. Mrs Peacock always loved anything about homicidal maniacs.

Once I picked up the paper and looked hard at the picture. 'Do you think she looks something like me?' I asked Mrs Peacock, and Mrs Peacock leaned back and looked at me and then at the picture and then at me again and finally she shook her head and said, 'No. If you wore your hair longer, and curlier, and your face was maybe a little fuller, there might be a little resemblance, but then if you looked like a homicidal maniac I wouldn't ever of let you in my house.'

'I think she kind of looks like me,' I said.

'You get along to work and stop being vain,' Mrs Peacock told me.

Of course when I got on the train with my round-trip ticket I had no idea how soon they'd be following me, and I suppose it was just as well, because it might have made me nervous and I might have done something wrong and spoiled everything. I knew that as soon as they gave up the notion that I was coming back to Rockville with my round-trip ticket they would think of Crain, which is the largest city that train went to, so I only stayed in Crain part of one day. I went to a big department store where they were having a store-wide sale; I figured that would land me in a crowd of shoppers and I was right; for a while there was a good chance that I'd never get any farther away from home than the ground floor of that department store in Crain. I had to fight my way through the crowd until I found the counter where they were having a sale of raincoats, and then I had to push and elbow down the counter and finally grab the raincoat I wanted right out of the hands of some old monster who couldn't have used it anyway because she was much too fat. You would have thought she had already paid for it, the way she howled. I was smart enough to have the exact change, all six dollars and eighty-nine cents, right in my hand, and I gave it to the salesgirl, grabbed the raincoat and the bag she wanted to put it in, and fought my way out again before I got crushed to death.

That raincoat was worth every cent of the six dollars and eighty-nine cents; I wore it right through until winter that year and not even a button ever came off it. I finally lost it the next spring when I left it somewhere and never got it back. It was tan, and the minute I put it on in the ladies' room of the store I began thinking of it as my 'old' raincoat; that was good. I had never before owned a raincoat like that and my mother would have fainted dead away. One thing I did that I thought

Louisa, Please Come Home

was kind of clever. I had left home wearing a light short coat; almost a jacket, and when I put on the raincoat of course I took off my light coat. Then all I had to do was empty the pockets of the light coat into the raincoat and carry the light coat casually over to a counter where they were having a sale of jackets and drop it on the counter as though I'd taken it off a little way to look at it and had decided against it. As far as I ever knew no one paid the slightest attention to me, and before I left the counter I saw a woman pick up my jacket and look it over; I could have told her she was getting a bargain for three ninety-eight.

It made me feel good to know that I had gotten rid of the light coat. My mother picked it out for me and even though I liked it and it was expensive it was also recognizable and I had to change it somehow. I was sure that if I put it in a bag and dropped it into a river or into a garbage truck of something like that sooner or later it would be found and even if no one saw me doing it, it would almost certainly be found, and then they would know I had changed my clothes in Crain.

That light coat never turned up. The last they ever found of me was someone in Rockville who caught a glimpse of me in the train station in Crain, and she recognized me by the light coat. They never found out where I went after that; it was partly luck and partly my clever planning. Two or three days later the papers were still reporting that I was in Crain; people thought they saw me on the streets and one girl who went into a store to buy a dress was picked up by the police and held until she could get someone to identify her. They were really looking, but they were looking for Louisa Tether, and I had stopped being Louisa Tether the minute I got rid of that light coat my mother bought me.

One thing I was relying on: there must be thousands of girls in the country on any given day who are nineteen years old, fair-haired, five feet four inches tall, and weighing one hundred and twenty-six pounds. And if there are thousands of girls like that, there must be, among those thousands, a good number who are wearing shapeless tan raincoats; I started counting tan raincoats in Crain after I left the department store and I passed four in one block, so I felt well hidden. After that I made myself even more invisible by doing just what I told my mother I was going to – I stopped in and had a sandwich in a little coffee shop, and then I went to a movie. I wasn't in any hurry at all, and rather than try to find a place to sleep that night I thought I would sleep on the train.

It's funny how no one pays any attention to you at all. There were hundreds of people who saw me that day, and even a sailor who tried to pick me up in the movie, and yet no one really *saw* me. If I had tried to check into a hotel the desk clerk might have noticed me, or if I had tried to get dinner in some fancy restaurant in that cheap raincoat I would have been conspicuous, but I was doing what any other girl looking like me and dressed like me might be doing that day. The only person who might be apt to remember me would be the man selling tickets in the railroad station, because girls

Louisa, Please Come Home

looking like me in old raincoats didn't buy train tickets, usually, at eleven at night, but I had thought of that, too, of course; I bought a ticket to Amityville, sixty miles away, and what made Amityville a perfectly reasonable disguise is that at Amityville there is a college, not a little fancy place like the one I had left so recently with nobody's blessing, but a big sprawling friendly affair, where my raincoat would look perfectly at home. I told myself I was a student coming back to the college after a week end at home. We got to Amityville after midnight, but it still didn't look odd when I left the train and went into the station, because while I was in the station, having a cup of coffee and killing time, seven other girls – I counted – wearing raincoats like mine came in or went out, not seeming to think it the least bit odd to be getting on or off trains at that hour of the night. Some of them had suitcases, and I wished that I had had some way of getting a suitcase in Crain, but it would have made me noticeable in the movie, and college girls going home for week ends often don't bother; they have pajamas and an extra pair of stockings at home, and they drop a toothbrush into one of the pockets of those invaluable raincoats. So I didn't worry about the suitcase then, although I knew I would need one soon. While I was having my coffee I made my own mind change from the idea that I was a college girl coming back after a week end at home to the idea that I was a college girl who was on her way home for a few days; all the time I tried to think as much as possible like what I was pretending to be, and after all, I *had* been a college girl for a while. I was thinking that even now the letter was in the mail, traveling as fast as the US Government could make it go, right to my father to tell him why I wasn't a college student any more; I suppose that was what finally decided me to run away, the thought of what my father would think and say and do when he got that letter from the college.

That was in the paper, too. They decided that the college business was the reason for my running away, but if that had been all, I don't think I would have left. No, I had been wanting to leave for so long, ever since I can remember, making plans till I was sure they were foolproof, and that's the way they turned out to be.

Sitting there in the station at Amityville, I tried to think myself into a good reason why I was leaving college to go home on a Monday night late, when I would hardly be going home for the week end. As I say, I always tried to think as hard as I could the way that suited whatever I wanted to be, and I liked to have a good reason for what I was doing. Nobody ever asked me, but it was good to know that I could answer them if they did. I finally decided that my sister was getting married the next day and I was going home at the beginning of the week to be one of her bridesmaids. I thought that was funny. I didn't want to be going home for any sad or frightening reason, like my mother being sick, or my father being hurt in a car accident, because I would have to look sad, and that might attract attention. So I was going home for my sister's wedding. I wandered around the station as though I had nothing to do, and just happened to pass the door when another girl was going out; she had on a raincoat just like mine and anyone who happened to notice would have thought that it was me who went out. Before I bought my ticket I went into the ladies' room and got another twenty dollars out of my shoe. I had nearly three hundred dollars left of the money I had taken from my father's desk and I had most of it in my shoes because I honestly couldn't think of another safe place to carry it. All I kept in my pocketbook was just enough for whatever I had to spend next. It's uncomfortable walking around all day on a wad of bills in your shoe, but they were good solid shoes, the kind of comfortable old shoes you wear whenever you don't really care how you look, and I had put new shoelaces in them before I left home so I could tie them good and tight. You can see, I planned pretty carefully, and no little detail got left out. If they had let me plan my sister's wedding there would have been a lot less of that running around and screaming and hysterics.

I bought a ticket to Chandler, which is the biggest city in this part of the state, and the place I'd been heading for all along. It was a good place to hide because people from Rockville tended to bypass it unless they had some special reason for going there – if they couldn't find the doctors or orthodontists or psychoanalysts or dress material they wanted in Rockville or Crain, they went directly to one of the really big cities, like the state capital; Chandler was big enough to hide in, but not big enough to look like a metropolis to people from

Rockville. The ticket seller in the Amityville station must have seen a good many college girls buying tickets for Chandler at all hours of the day or night because he took my money and shoved the ticket at me without even looking up.

Funny. They must have come looking for me in Chandler at some time or other, because it's not likely they would have neglected any possible place I might be, but maybe Rockville people never seriously believed that anyone would go to Chandler from choice, because I never felt for a minute that anyone was looking for me there. My picture was in the Chandler papers, of course, but as far as I ever knew no one ever looked at me twice, and I got up every morning and went to work and went shopping in the stores and went to movies with Mrs Peacock and went out to the beach all that summer without ever being afraid of being recognized. I behaved just like everyone else, and dressed just like everyone else, and even *thought* just like everyone else, and the only person I ever saw from Rockville in three years was a friend of my mother's, and I knew *she* only came to Chandler to get her poodle bred at the kennels there. She didn't look as if she was in a state to recognize anybody but another poodle-fancier, anyway, and all I had to do was step into a doorway as she went by, and she never looked at me.

Two other college girls got on the train to Chandler when I did; maybe both of them were going home for their sisters' weddings. Neither of them was wearing a tan raincoat, but one of them had on an old blue jacket that gave the same general effect. I fell asleep as soon as the train started, and once I woke up and for a minute I wondered where I was and then I realized that I was doing it, I was actually carrying out my careful plan and had gotten better than halfway with it, and I almost laughed, there in the train with everyone asleep around me. Then I went back to sleep and didn't wake up until we got into Chandler about seven in the morning.

So there I was. I had left home just after lunch the day before, and now at seven in the morning of my sister's wedding day I was so far away, in every sense, that I *knew* they would never find me. I had all day to get myself settled in Chandler, so I started off by having breakfast in a restaurant near the station, and then went off to find a place to live, and a job. The first thing I did was buy a suitcase, and it's funny how people don't really notice you if you're buying a suitcase near a railroad station. Suitcases look *natural* near railroad stations, and I picked out one of those stores that sell a little bit of everything, and bought a cheap suitcase and a pair of stockings and some handkerchiefs and a little traveling clock, and I put everything into the suitcase and carried that. Nothing is hard to do unless you get upset or excited about it.

Later on, when Mrs Peacock and I used to read in the papers about my disappearing, I asked her once if she thought that Louisa Tether had gotten as far as Chandler and she didn't.

'They're saying now she was kidnapped,' Mrs Peacock told me, 'and that's what I think happened. Kidnapped, and murdered, and they do *terrible* things to young girls they kidnap.'

'But the papers say there wasn't any ransom note.'

'That's what they *say*.' Mrs Peacock shook her head at me. 'How do we know what the family is keeping secret? Or if she was kidnapped by a homicidal maniac, why should *he* send a ransom note? Young girls like you don't know a lot of the things that go on, I can tell you.'

'I feel kind of sorry for the girl,' I said.

'You can't ever tell,' Mrs Peacock said. 'Maybe she went with him willingly.'

I didn't know, that first morning in Chandler, that Mrs Peacock was going to turn up that first day, the luckiest thing that ever happened to me. I decided while I was having breakfast that I was going to be a nineteen-year-old girl from upstate with a nice family and a good background who had been saving money to come to Chandler and take a secretarial course in the business school there. I was going to have to find some kind of a job to keep on earning money while I went to school; courses at the business school wouldn't start until fall, so I would have the summer to work and save money and decide if I really wanted to take secretarial training. If I decided not to stay in Chandler I could easily go somewhere else after the fuss about my running away had died down. The raincoat looked wrong for the kind of conscientious young girl I was going to be, so I took it off and carried it over my arm. I think I did a pretty good job on my clothes, altogether. Before I left home I decided that I would have to wear a suit, as quiet and unobtrusive as I could find, and I picked out a gray suit, with a white blouse, so with just one or two small changes like a different blouse or some kind of a pin on the lapel, I could look like whoever I decided to be. Now the suit looked absolutely right for a young girl planning to take a secretarial course, and I looked like a thousand other people when I walked down the street carrying my suitcase and my raincoat over my arm; people get off trains every minute looking just like that. I bought a morning paper and stopped in a drugstore for a cup of coffee and a look to see the rooms for rent. It was all so usual – suitcase, coat, rooms for rent – that when I asked the soda clerk how to get to Primrose Street he never even looked at me. He certainly didn't care whether I ever got to Primrose Street or not, but he told me very politely where it was and what bus to take. I didn't really need to take the bus for economy, but it would have looked funny for a girl who was saving money to arrive in a taxi.

'I'll never forget how you looked that first morning,' Mrs Peacock told me once, much later. 'I knew right away you were the kind of girl I like to rent rooms to – quiet, and well-mannered. But you looked almighty scared of the big city.'

'I wasn't scared,' I said. 'I was worried about finding a nice room. My mother told me so many things to be careful about I was afraid I'd never find anything to suit her.'

'*Any*body's mother could come into my house at any time and know that her daughter was in good hands,' Mrs Peacock said, a little huffy.

But it was true. When I walked into Mrs Peacock's rooming house on Primrose Street, and met Mrs Peacock, I knew that I couldn't have done this part better if I'd been able to plan it. The house was old, and comfortable, and my room was nice, and Mrs Peacock and I hit it off right away. She was very pleased with me when she heard that my mother had told me to be sure the room I found was clean and that the neighborhood was good, with no chance of rowdies following a girl if she came home after dark, and she was even more pleased when she heard that I wanted to save money and take a secretarial course so I could get a really good job and earn enough to be able to send a little home every week; Mrs Peacock believed that children owed it to their parents to pay back some of what had been spent on them while they were growing up. By the time I had been in the house an hour Mrs Peacock knew all about my imaginary family upstate: my mother, who was a widow, and my sister, who had just gotten married and still lived at my mother's home with her husband, and my young brother Paul, who worried my mother a good deal because he didn't seem to want to settle down. My name was Lois Taylor, I told her. By that time, I think I could have told her my real name and she would never have connected it with the girl

Louisa, Please Come Home

in the paper, because by then she was feeling that she almost knew my family, and she wanted me to be sure and tell my mother when I wrote home that Mrs Peacock would make herself personally responsible for me while I was in the city and take as good care of me as my own mother would. On top of everything else, she told me that a stationery store in the neighborhood was looking for a girl assistant, and there I was. Before I had been away from home for twenty-four hours I was an entirely new person. I was a girl named Lois Taylor who lived on Primrose Street and worked down at the stationery store.

I read in the papers one day about how a famous fortune-teller wrote to my father offering to find me and said that astral signs had convinced him that I would be found near flowers. That gave me a jolt, because of Primrose Street, but my father and Mrs Peacock and the rest of the world thought that it meant that my body was buried somewhere. They dug up a vacant lot near the railroad station where I was last seen, and Mrs Peacock was very disappointed when nothing turned up. Mrs Peacock and I could not decide whether I had run away with a gangster to be a gun moll, or whether my body had been cut up and sent somewhere in a trunk. After a while they stopped looking for me, except for an occasional false clue that would turn up in a small story on the back pages of the paper, and Mrs Peacock and I got interested in the stories about a daring daylight bank robbery in Chicago. When the anniversary of my running away came around, and I realized that

I had really been gone for a year, I treated myself to a new hat and dinner downtown, and came home just in time for the evening news broadcast and my mother's voice over the radio.

'Louisa,' she was saying, 'please come home.'

'That poor poor woman,' Mrs Peacock said. 'Imagine how she must feel. They say she's never given up hope of finding her little girl alive someday.'

'Do you like my new hat?' I asked her.

I had given up all idea of the secretarial course because the stationery store had decided to expand and include a lending library and a gift shop, and I was now the manager of the gift shop and if things kept on well would someday be running the whole thing; Mrs Peacock and I talked it over, just as if she had been my mother, and we decided that I would be foolish to leave a good job to start over somewhere else. The money that I had been saving was in the bank, and Mrs Peacock and I thought that one of these days we might pool our savings and buy a little car, or go on a trip somewhere, or even a cruise.

What I am saying is that I was free, and getting along fine, with never a thought that I knew about ever going back. It was just plain rotten bad luck that I had to meet Paul. I had gotten so I hardly ever thought about any of them any more, and never wondered what they were doing unless I happened to see some item in the papers, but there must have been something in the back of my mind remembering them all the time because I never even stopped to think; I just stood there on the street

Louisa, Please Come Home

with my mouth open, and said '*Paul!*' He turned around and then of course I realized what I had done, but it was too late. He stared at me for a minute, and then frowned, and then looked puzzled; I could see him first trying to remember, and then trying to believe what he remembered; at last he said, 'Is it possible?'

He said I had to go back. He said if I didn't go back he would tell them where to come and get me. He also patted me on the head and told me that there was still a reward waiting there in the bank for anyone who turned up with conclusive news of me, and he said that after he had collected the reward I was perfectly welcome to run away again, as far and as often as I liked.

Maybe I did want to go home. Maybe all that time I had been secretly waiting for a chance to get back; maybe that's why I recognized Paul on the street, in a coincidence that wouldn't have happened once in a million years – he had never even *been* to Chandler before, and was only there for a few minutes between trains; he had stepped out of the station for a minute, and found me. If I had not been passing at that minute, if he had stayed in the station where he belonged, I would never have gone back. I told Mrs Peacock I was going home to visit my family upstate. I thought that was funny.

Paul sent a telegram to my mother and father, saying that he had found me, and we took a plane back; Paul said he was still afraid that I'd try to get away again and the safest place for me was high up in the air where he knew I couldn't get off and run.

I began to get nervous, looking out the taxi window on

the way from the Rockville airport; I would have sworn that for three years I hadn't given a thought to that town, to those streets and stores and houses I used to know so well, but here I found that I remembered it all, as though I hadn't ever seen Chandler and *its* houses and streets; it was almost as though I had never been away at all. When the taxi finally turned the corner into my own street, and I saw the big old white house again, I almost cried.

'Of course I wanted to come back,' I said, and Paul laughed. I thought of the return-trip ticket I had kept as a lucky charm for so long, and how I had thrown it away one day when I was emptying my pocketbook; I wondered when I threw it away whether I would ever want to go back and regret throwing away my ticket. 'Everything looks just the same,' I said. 'I caught the bus right there on the corner; I came down the driveway that day and met you.'

'If I had managed to stop you that day,' Paul said, 'you would probably never have tried again.'

Then the taxi stopped in front of the house and my knees were shaking when I got out. I grabbed Paul's arm and said, 'Paul . . . wait a minute,' and he gave me a look I used to know very well, a look that said 'If you back out on me now I'll see that you never forget it,' and put his arm around me because I was shivering and we went up the walk to the front door.

I wondered if they were watching us from the window. It was hard for me to imagine how my mother and father would behave in a situation like this, because they always made such a point of being quiet and dignified and proper; I thought that Mrs Peacock would have been halfway down the walk to meet us, but here the front door ahead was still tight shut. I wondered if we would have to ring the doorbell; I had never had to ring this doorbell before. I was still wondering when Carol opened the door for us. 'Carol!' I said. I was shocked because she looked so old, and then I thought that of course it had been three years since I had seen her and she probably thought that *I* looked older, too. 'Carol,' I said, 'Oh, Carol!' I was honestly glad to see her.

She looked at me hard and then stepped back and my mother and father were standing there, waiting for me to come in. If I had not stopped to think I would have run to them, but I hesitated, not quite sure what to do, or whether they were angry with me, or hurt, or only just happy that I was back, and of course once I stopped to think about it all I could find to do was just stand there and say 'Mother?' kind of uncertainly.

She came over to me and put her hands on my shoulders and looked into my face for a long time. There were tears running down her cheeks and I thought that before, when it didn't matter, I had been ready enough to cry, but now, when crying would make me look better, all I wanted to do was giggle. She looked old, and sad, and I felt simply foolish. Then she turned to Paul and said, 'Oh, *Paul* – how can you do this to me again?'

Paul was frightened; I could see it. 'Mrs Tether –' he said.

'What is your name, dear?' my mother asked me.

'Louisa Tether,' I said stupidly.

'No, dear,' she said, very gently, 'your *real* name?'

Now I could cry, but now I did not think it was going to help matters any. 'Louisa Tether,' I said. 'That's my name.'

'Why don't you people leave us alone?' Carol said; she was white, and shaking, and almost screaming because she was so angry. 'We've spent years and years trying to find my lost sister and all people like you see in it is a chance to cheat us out of the reward – doesn't it mean *any*thing to you that *you* may think you have a chance for some easy money, but we just get hurt and heartbroken all over again? Why don't you leave us *alone*?'

'Carol,' my father said, 'you're frightening the poor child. Young lady,' he said to me, 'I honestly believe that you did not realize the cruelty of what you tried to do. You look like a nice girl; try to imagine your own mother –'

I tried to imagine my own mother; I looked straight at her.

'– if someone took advantage of her like this. I am sure you were not told that twice before, this young man –' I stopped looking at my mother and looked at Paul – 'has brought us young girls who pretended to be our lost daughter; each time he protested that he had been genuinely deceived and had no thought of profit, and each time we hoped desperately that it would be the right girl. The first time we were taken in for several days. The girl *looked* like our Louisa, she *acted* like our Louisa, she knew all kinds of small family jokes and happenings it seemed impossible that anyone *but*

Louisa, Please Come Home

Louisa could know, and yet she was an imposter. And the girl's mother – my wife – has suffered more each time her hopes have been raised.' He put his arm around my mother – his wife – and with Carol they stood all together looking at me.

'Look,' Paul said wildly, 'give her a *chance* – she *knows* she's Louisa. At least give her a chance to *prove* it.'

'How?' Carol asked. 'I'm sure if I asked her something like – well – like what was the color of the dress she was supposed to wear at my wedding –'

'It was pink,' I said. 'I wanted blue but you said it had to be pink.'

'I'm sure she'd know the answer,' Carol went on as though I hadn't said anything. 'The other girls you brought here, Paul – *they* both knew.'

It wasn't going to be any good. I ought to have known it. Maybe they were so used to looking for me by now that they would rather keep on looking than have me home; maybe once my mother had looked in my face and seen there nothing of Louisa, but only the long careful concentration I had put into being Lois Taylor, there was never any chance of my looking like Louisa again.

I felt kind of sorry for Paul; he had never understood them as well as I did and he clearly felt there was still some chance of talking them into opening their arms and crying out 'Louisa! Our long-lost daughter!' and then turning around and handing him the reward; after that, we could all live happily ever after. While Paul was still trying to argue with my father I walked over a little way and looked into the living room again; I figured I wasn't going to have much time to look around and I wanted one last glimpse to take away with me; sister Carol kept a good eye on me all the time, too. *I* wondered what the two girls before me had tried to steal, and I wanted to tell her that if *I* ever planned to steal anything from that house I was three years too late; I could have taken whatever I wanted when I left the first time. There was nothing there I could take now, any more than there had been before. I realized that all I wanted was to stay –I wanted to stay so much that I felt like hanging onto the stair rail and screaming, but even though a temper tantrum might bring them some fleeting recollection of their dear lost Louisa I hardly thought it would persuade them to invite me to stay. I could just picture myself being dragged kicking and screaming out of my own house.

'Such a lovely old house,' I said politely to my sister Carol, who was hovering around me.

'Our family has lived here for generations,' she said, just as politely.

'Such beautiful furniture,' I said.

'My mother is fond of antiques.'

'Fingerprints,' Paul was shouting. We were going to get a lawyer, I gathered, or at least Paul thought we were going to get a lawyer and I wondered how he was going to feel when he found out that we weren't. I couldn't imagine any lawyer in the world who could get my mother and my father and my sister Carol to take me back when they had made up their minds that I was not

Louisa; could the law make my mother look into my face and recognize me?

I thought that there ought to be some way I could make Paul see that there was nothing we could do, and I came over and stood next to him. 'Paul,' I said, 'can't you see that you're only making Mr Tether angry?'

'Correct, young woman,' my father said, and nodded at me to show that he thought I was being a sensible creature. 'He's not doing himself any good by threatening me.'

'Paul,' I said, 'these people don't want us here.'

Paul started to say something and then for the first time in his life thought better of it and stamped off toward the door. When I turned to follow him – thinking that we'd never gotten past the front hall in my great homecoming – my father – excuse me, Mr Tether – came up behind me and took my hand. 'My daughter was younger than you are,' he said to me very kindly, 'but I'm sure you have a family somewhere who love you and want you to be happy. Go back to them, young lady. Let me advise you as though I were really your father – stay away from that fellow, he's wicked and he's worthless. Go back home where you belong.'

'We know what it's like for a family to worry and wonder about a daughter,' my mother said. 'Go back to the people who love you.'

That meant Mrs Peacock, I guess.

'Just to make sure you get there,' my father said, 'let us help toward your fare.' I tried to take my hand away, but he put a folded bill into it and I had to take it. 'I hope someday,' he said, 'that someone will do as much for our Louisa.'

'Good-by, my dear,' my mother said, and she reached up and patted my cheek. 'Very good luck to you.'

'I hope your daughter comes back someday,' I told them. 'Good-by.'

The bill was a twenty, and I gave it to Paul. It seemed little enough for all the trouble he had taken and, after all, I could go back to my job in the stationery store. My mother still talks to me on the radio, once a year, on the anniversary of the day I ran away.

'Louisa,' she says, 'Please come home. We all want our dear girl back, and we need you and miss you so much. Your mother and father love you and will never forget you. Louisa, please come home.'

PENGUIN ARCHIVE

H. G. Wells *The Time Machine*
M. R. James *The Stalls of Barchester Cathedral*
Jane Austen *The History of England by a Partial, Prejudiced and Ignorant Historian*
Edgar Allan Poe *Hop-Frog*
Virginia Woolf *The New Dress*
Antoine de Saint-Exupéry *Night Flight*
Oscar Wilde *A Poet Can Survive Everything But a Misprint*
George Orwell *Can Socialists be Happy?*
Dorothy Parker *Horsie*
D. H. Lawrence *Odour of Chrysanthemums*
Homer *The Wrath of Achilles*
Emily Brontë *No Coward Soul Is Mine*
Romain Gary *Lady L.*
Charles Dickens *The Chimes*
Dante *Hell*
Georges Simenon *Stan the Killer*
F. Scott Fitzgerald *The Rich Boy*
Katherine Mansfield *A Dill Pickle*
Fyodor Dostoyevsky *The Dream of a Ridiculous Man*

Franz Kafka *A Hunger-Artist*
Leo Tolstoy *Family Happiness*
Karen Blixen *The Dreaming Child*
Federico García Lorca *Cicada!*
Vladimir Nabokov *Revenge*
Albert Camus *A Short Guide to Towns Without a Past*
Muriel Spark *The Driver's Seat*
Carson McCullers *Reflections in a Golden Eye*
Wu Cheng'en *Monkey King Makes Havoc in Heaven*
Friedrich Nietzsche *Ecce Homo*
Laurie Lee *A Moment of War*
Roald Dahl *Lamb to the Slaughter*
Frank O'Connor *The Genius*
James Baldwin *The Fire Next Time*
Hermann Hesse *Strange News from Another Planet*
Gertrude Stein *Paris France*
Seneca *Why I am a Stoic*
Snorri Sturluson *The Prose Edda*
Elizabeth Gaskell *Lois the Witch*
Sei Shōnagon *A Lady in Kyoto*
Yasunari Kawabata *Thousand Cranes*
Jack Kerouac *Tristessa*
Arthur Schnitzler *A Confirmed Bachelor*
Chester Himes *All God's Chillun Got Pride*

Bram Stoker *The Burial of the Rats*
Czesław Miłosz *Rescue*
Hans Christian Andersen *The Emperor's New Clothes*
Bohumil Hrabal *Closely Watched Trains*
Italo Calvino *Under the Jaguar Sun*
Stanislaw Lem *The Seventh Voyage*
Shirley Jackson *The Daemon Lover*
Stefan Zweig *Chess*
Kate Chopin *The Story of an Hour*
Allen Ginsberg *Sunflower Sutra*
Rabindranath Tagore *The Broken Nest*
Søren Kierkegaard *The Seducer's Diary*
Mary Shelley *Transformation*
Nikolai Leskov *Night Owls*
Willa Cather *A Lost Lady*
Emilia Pardo Bazán *The Lady Bandit*
W. B. Yeats *Sailing to Byzantium*
Margaret Cavendish *The Blazing World*
Lafcadio Hearn *Some Japanese Ghosts*
Sarah Orne Jewett *The Country of the Pointed Firs*
Vincent van Gogh *For Art and for Life*
Dylan Thomas *Do Not Go Gentle Into That Good Night*
Mikhail Bulgakov *A Dog's Heart*
Saadat Hasan Manto *The Price of Freedom*

Gérard de Nerval *October Nights*
Rumi *Where Everything is Music*
H. P. Lovecraft *The Shadow Out of Time*
Christina Rossetti *To Read and Dream*
Dambudzo Marechera *The House of Hunger*
Andy Warhol *Beauty*
Maurice Leblanc *The Escape of Arsène Lupin*
Eileen Chang *Jasmine Tea*
Irmgard Keun *After Midnight*
Walter Benjamin *Unpacking My Library*
Epictetus *Whatever is Rational is Tolerable*
Ota Pavel *How I Came to Know Fish*
César Aira *An Episode in the Life of a Landscape Painter*
Hafez *I am a Bird from Paradise*
Clarice Lispector *The Burned Sinner and the Harmonious Angels*
Maryse Condé *Tales from the Heart*
Audre Lorde *Coal*
Mary Gaitskill *Secretary*
Tove Ditlevsen *The Umbrella*
June Jordan *Passion*
Antonio Tabucchi *Requiem*
Alexander Lernet-Holenia *Baron Bagge*
Wang Xiaobo *The Maverick Pig*